MW00380658

Run

Table of Contents

Chapter 1: The Beginning

My name is Jabari Wilson, a 17 year old kid who was in the wrong place at the wrong time. See I was what they call a 'good kid'; I got straight A's in school with a 4.0 GPA and always have throughout grade school, middle school, and now high school. I was captain of both the football and basketball teams, a quarterback in the former and a point guard in the latter, and generally, I didn't cause trouble and have never gotten detention, suspended, or any kind of punishment in school.

To describe myself, my appearance, I'd say that I was good-looking, 5ft 11 inches tall with dark brown skin, an afro, and a nice mustache growing. My build is somewhat athletic, though on the skinny side, though I still managed to be one of the stronger and faster kids on both of my teams. I lived with my mother and father in a relatively small apartment downtown, along with my younger 14 year old brother Jaheem. Jaheem followed in my footsteps except he was more aggressive, less willing to listen to others, and had occasionally gotten in trouble for back talking to teachers and other authority figures. Jaheem was a bit shorter, 5ft 8 inches in height, and was a shade lighter than me. He had his hair cornrowed and was skinnier than I was, even at that age.

Me and my brother were close, we hung out all the time, played video games together, talked about life, etc. I even drove him to school and picked him up whenever he needed it. Life was good, and I was on the path to become something special, possibly division 1 in both sports, getting a full ride to college, I was set. My future was bright.

In other words, I've never gotten in trouble, I've never done anything wrong before, so it was a shock when one day me and my younger brother were stopped by the police.

It was a fairly normal day, the weather was nice, and me and Jaheem were driving to the store to pick up some snacks, a drink, and some batteries. We were hungry and craving some sugar mostly, and the house was running low on batteries which were used for things like remote controls, flashlights, my electric razor, my electric toothbrush, and so on. We weren't completely out yet, but better to be safe than sorry. So we were riding along in my red 2016 Chevy Impala with the black interior, just talking about basketball and girls.

"I'm telling you 'Heem, the most important thing you need to truly be great, is handles." I spoke, discussing with Jaheem the intricacies of basketball.

"Nah, kill that noise bruh. Handles? Get all the way out of here. You need a jumpshot first and foremost. And to supplement that, next is defense. Handles doesn't even come into the equation." He responded, looking at me as if I was crazy.

"Really? With handle, you turnover the ball less, you can run fast breaks, get to the hole easier, break a team down with your skills alone, and you're impossible to guard one on one. A jumpshot can be shut down by any decent defender just staying in front of you, getting a hand in your face. And defense is good, but most defensive players aren't even well known or good in anyway." I countered, defending my decision.

"I got one word for that. Picks. Let's say you can guard me so well, that I never get off a shot. I just simply pass the ball away and/or get a screen from one of my teammates, leaving you lagging behind and me open for the buckets." He said, mimicking the shot of a basketball player.

"Alright watch your hands, we're not trying to get in an accident." I warned him.

"And ," He begins, ignoring my warning, "if I can shoot, that means 3's. And obviously 3's outclass anything you can do with handle no question. You hit 8 layups by breaking the defense down? OK, you got 16 points. I hit eight 3's and I got 24 points. Not even close. We can even make it more even and I only hit one 3 pointer out of my 8 made shots, and still I have 17 AKA more than you. Just face it, a jumpshot's better in every way." He argued once more.

"Yeah well—" I began before suddenly slamming on the brakes. While we had the right of way and the green light, the car across the lane (a moderate sized black truck) and on the right (my left) had still turned suddenly, nearly causing an accident. If I had kept going, as I had the right to, we would've either crashed or gotten within inches of doing so. Reckless.

"Damn. People can't drive for nothing." Commented my brother, the sudden stop causing him to lurch forward a bit, though he was held back by his seat belt. Wasn't that the truth? I always noticed despite driving well enough to pass their driving test, most people totally switched gears (pun intended) once they got out on the open road. No regard for the rules, for common courtesy, or common sense at all. It seemed like people were willing to crash and/or possibly die for their right to drive terrible. It made no sense. That's why I always preached safe and cautious driving.

"Yeah man. That's why I tell you, you got to be careful when driving. No matter how well you drive and how well you follow the rules, there's always someone driving stupid out here, ready to cause an accident. You just got to be aware and act accordingly." I explained, looking around for any more sudden cars, before continuing to the store.

"So enough about basketball, let's talk about something else. I can clearly see that you're too stuck on the importance of a jumpshot, acting like most great shooters aren't simply roleplayers. So let's move on." I requested, throwing one last argument in there.

"And I can see you're ignoring all the point guards with crazy amounts of handle that go absolutely nowhere. Really you're talking about what YOU need more to play basketball, because you're already fast and strong, and handles makes you nearly unstoppable." Jaheem exclaimed. "And how're you going to call for a change in subject and try to make some last ditch argument on it. That doesn't even make sense." He added.

"Well I did, so let's move on. How about girls? I notice you talking to girls more and more when I pick you up. How's that going, you got a girlfriend yet?" I half asked, half teased my brother. I really have noticed a big change in him though. Over the last few months, I've always seen him trying to spit game to a girl before I come pick him up. Sometimes I even wait a few minutes until it looks like he's kind of lost, before showing up to save him. Don't get me wrong, talking to girls is fine, more than fine actually; I just want to see where his head's at and make sure he doesn't get too caught up in it.

"Yeah I'm talking to girls more, and nah I don't got a girlfriend yet. What about you, how's Nia?" He asked, turning the question back on me. Nia was a girl that was in a lot of my honor roll and AP classes. She was one of the top students, behind only myself, and still was beautiful to boot. 5'5", brown eyes, black braided hair (all natural too), a nice figure, she was a good pick. That's why I made her my girlfriend.

"She's good. But we're not talking about me and Nia, we're talking about you and your girl issues." I retorted, changing the subject from Nia back to 'Heem. Me and her were good, so that didn't need any discussion. We chilled from time to time, did homework together, and the relationship was fine. 'Heem on the other hand...

"Issues? Man I'm good with the girls. I don't know what 'issues' you're talking about." He replied, face scrunching up at the perceived insult. I mean it wasn't *really* an insult. Just an observation mixed with some teasing. I'm sure he'd do fine eventually, but watching him flounder like that was still hilarious on all levels. But for now, I had to calm him down and stop him from catching feelings.

"Not like that 'Heem, no diss. I'm just saying, you seem to be talking to girls more and I'm trying to see where your head's at. Are you just doing it for fun? Looking for a girlfriend? Trying just to smash? And depending on those answers, I got to make sure you're handling yourself right as to not cause problems for yourself down the line." I said, informing him of my motives. It's hard to tell these days. Most boys pretend they're just trying to smash girls nonstop like they're Hulk or something, but the large majority of them don't

4

even touch a girl. Then there are boys who actually mean it, and then some who only want a girlfriend. In my opinion he didn't really need to focus on them much. He was still too young.

"Oh, alright then. Right now I'm just having fun, shopping around, know what I mean? As for smashing and 'handling myself right', don't worry Fam, I got this. I know what you 'bout to say about condoms and being safe, blah blah blah. I'm good. I know." He stated. I know he did, with how much I pushed condoms and safe sex and the idea of not just smashing any random girl. I basically burrowed it into his brain with how much I stressed it.

"Yeah but there's more to it than that. I'd also say that you should pick and choose who you smash. I'm not saying to save yourself for abstinence or nothing like that, but make sure she's worthy of you." I replied back, looking my brother in his eyes as we're at a red light. He looked back at me for a second, nodding his head as he seemed to get what I was saying.

"Yeah I see what you're saying. Be selective and stuff. I'm not trying to be a man whore or nothing, believe that, so I see what you're saying. Like I said before, I'm good." He proclaimed. That worked for me. I just wanted him to be aware of how to conduct himself and protect himself properly. It was my job as the older brother to pass down my knowledge to him and protect him in life, and dealing with girls was no exception.

We drove another minute in silence, the scenery passing by in blurs, with a pretty much open road, before reaching the store.

"Alright, we're only here for snacks, drinks, and batteries. Try not to go crazy." I told him as I parked the car and started to unbuckle my seat belt. He said nothing and just gave me a look of annoyance as we entered the store. We separated immediately, him going for the snacks and drinks and me going for the batteries. I looked around the store, searching for batteries. First I looked in the back, near the random electronics that stores like this seemed to have, and then snaked my way up and down every aisle before finding them. They were near the register. Damn, I could've just gotten my snacks first and gotten the batteries after, basically making this a waste of time. Oh well, time spent and lesson learned. Well it's only been a few minutes, and with that taken care of, I could now go look at the snacks. As I walked towards the food aisles, I saw Jaheem, all ready to go with snacks in hand. My brother had some chips and a fruit punch in his hand, and was already basically at checkout so I felt rushed a bit to get something quickly. Peering around, I saw a multitude of candy from gummy worms, to flavored hard candy, to gum, to an entire section of chocolates, caramels, nuts, and so on. But what caught my eye most was a chocolate and peanut butter candy bar. Swiftly I picked that up along with a bottle of water I had seen earlier to drink. Despite the rush I probably picked the better option between us (a healthier choice definitely. Plus sweets tend to taste better than whatever chips are), so I was good.

I walked up to the register, put my candy, batteries, and water down, and handed a five dollar bill to the girl at the register. I looked around as the cashier processed my purchase, and panicked for a second when I didn't see my brother. Luckily I could look through the window and see that he was waiting near the car. I thanked the cashier for the change she handed back to me, grabbed my bag, and made my way to the car as well. It only took me a few seconds to catch up to him, but of course my little brother had a lot to say.

"Damn, what took you so long? Getting batteries held you up that much?" Asked Jaheem, joking somewhat, yet clearly bored from his short time of waiting.

"Nah, it only took a second. Not my fault you shop at super speed." I replied, returning the joke.

"Super speed? That's just you being slow boy. Don't get salty 'cause you don't move with the swiftness like I do." He said smugly, as he opens the door to the car.

"Yeah, well watch your mouth before you end up walking home." I retorted, before opening my own door and starting the car. I sat down, buckled up, looked around to make sure Jaheem's buckled up too, looked for any oncoming drivers, and then took off. We rode in relative silence, Jaheem eating his chips and enjoying his snacks, while I focused on the road. We were about half way home when suddenly we heard a siren go "WOOP WOOP"; it was the sound of the police.

We both looked around vigorously, searching for something that the cop car could possibly be chasing. I didn't see anything, so I turned to Jaheem. He just shrugged and I pulled over to the side to let the police car through. Strangely when I did, the car followed me as if...I was the target. But that didn't make sense? I mean I didn't break any rules, run any stop signs, red lights, nothing. I looked over to Jaheem and saw that he had his seat belt on so that was covered. I looked down at myself and yep, I was buckled in too. What could he possibly want from us?

"Hey Jaheem, I think the cop's for us. It's pulling us over for some reason. You see anything?" I asked my brother.

"For us? Come on man, that doesn't make any sense. We ain't do nothing wrong!" He exclaimed, throwing his hands in the air.

"Exactly. So I suggest we just get this over with and talk to the officer. It's probably a misunderstanding." I reassured him.

"I don't know. I don't like this, it seems fishy. We should just drive home, wait until we get there. That's a thing you know, we don't HAVE to pull over here. At home there's less chance of...B.S. Happening." He

6

replied, clearly worried due to the less than stellar rep police had nowadays. Sure there were a few reports of police brutality and wrongdoings, but all cops couldn't be bad. He was overreacting.

"Look there's nothing to be afraid of. We've done nothing wrong, we're not threatening in any way, so they have no reason to get violent. Just listen to the officer and stay cool and we'll be off and driving back home in no time."

"I don't know man, I don't like it. That's all I'm saying."

"Don't worry. We'll be fine."

Chapter 2: Conflict

We both sat perfectly still for a while, just waiting for this to be over with before it even started. I took a deep breath and remembered what I'd heard about what to do when pulled over by the police. First thing was to be as non-threatening as possible. Slowly I reached over Jaheem to grab the registration for the car.

"Ay, yo what're you doing?" He asked, perturbed by me reaching across him, disturbing his personal space.

"I'm getting my license and registration out now. I'd rather not reach for things when the officer gets here." I informed him. "I'm not trying to get shot."

He just sat back and nodded with that response, allowing me to retrieve what I needed. Once I got the paperwork out, I reached into my pocket and got out my license and kept both that and the registration in my hands. I then placed both of my hands on the steering wheel, in sight, all accounted for. I wasn't taking any chances with this. It likely wasn't going to be an issue, but just in case. Speaking of that, I had to make sure Jaheem was straight too.

"Jaheem, make your hands visible on the glove compartment. We don't need to give them any reason to fear us." I informed him. He rolled his eyes but eventually did what I said, raising his hands in front of him, so that they could now be seen. If we made no threat to them, they'd be no threat to us.

We waited a few more minutes, and still the officer hadn't gotten out of the car yet. It was nerve wracking and unusual behavior. Add on Jaheem's attitude, where he was clearly prepared for a fight of some kind, and I couldn't help but to be nervous. With another deep breath, I let out all my worries. I was just being paranoid. Just calm down and it'd all be fine.

After another 3 minutes, the officer had finally gotten out of his car and had made his way towards our car. THUMP THUMP THUMP. He knocked on the window, beckoning me to take one of my hands and lower the window.

"There a problem officer?" I asked, sincere in my questioning. I really had no idea why he was pulling us over. He promptly ignored me as he looked in the car.

"License and registration." Is all he said, speaking with a stern tone of voice. Scary enough I could see that his hand was on his gun, and quickly looked away. Was I threatening him somehow? Did he see something he didn't like? I don't see why he needs his gun. Nonetheless, I slowly took my hand from the steering wheel and reached the officer exactly what he requested. Quickly the officer snatched the papers from my hand and began to look over it.

"So...how's the weather?" I asked, trying to make small talk. Nothing. The policeman didn't even budge or spare me a look as he continued peering over my documents. Okay, maybe a different question?

"How's your day been officer? Uneventful I hope?" I inquired with a smile. Again I got no reaction from the officer who was supernaturally focused on searching through my license and registration. Getting more serious and business like, I changed my line of questioning. Maybe he could shed some light on exactly why we were being pulled over.

"Officer, can I ask why we're being pulled over. Is there some type of issue?" I questioned one more time. Once again the officer was as quiet as a mouse.

"So no then!" Exclaimed Jaheem, exasperated at the situation. With his words, the officer immediately handed the papers back to me. I uttered a quick "thank you" as I accepted them.

"OK, I'm going to have to ask you to step out of the car. Both of you." Spoke the officer, his hand still on his gun.

"What? Why? For what reason? We did nothing wrong!" I exclaim. I was genuinely confused. Why would we have to get out of the car? He didn't even find anything wrong with the registration!

"Just get out of the car. Don't make this difficult *boy*!" Said the officer with a raised voice. As soon as he finished speaking, Jaheem went off.

"Oh hell no! He did NOT just say boy!" He yelled. "You better get your boy Jabari, or he's going to mess around and get these hands."

"Calm down Jaheem. Let's not make this worse." I told him, placing my hand on his left arm. "We're good."

"Calm down? CALM DOWN!? He's clearly on his racist tip at this point, profiling us simply because we're black. And we don't have to get out of the car unless he gives us a reason! I know my rights!" Yelled my brother, irate at the situation.

9

"Come on Jaheem, don't do this. Just comply with the officer's request and everything will be fine." I reassured him. Or tried to anyways. As I spoke, my brother looked hurt and somewhat defeated. He looked down for a second and then back up at me, sadness in his eyes.

"Why are you letting them do this to us?" He asked, the emotion clear in his voice. Such a simple question that I'd never be able to answer. Instead I chose not to and simply replied.

"We're not in trouble Jaheem. We did nothing wrong. Like I said, we're *good*. Don't worry." I said once more before slowly reaching down and unbuckling my seat belt. Calmly I reached over to the interior handle on the car door and stepped out of the car as the officer requested. Peculiarly, the officer's grip on his gun only tightened with my compliance. He then looked back at his car.

"Eric, I'm going to need some backup for these boys! They look like they might get violent!" The officer yelled at who I presumed was his partner. That was confusing as we've done nothing but listen to the officer. Why would he think we'd be violent? Clearly there was a misunderstanding here.

"Officer, I can assure you that we're not going to be violent at all. We just want to know why we're being arrested. That's all." I explained, hands up to better exemplify my position. Surely he could understand that we meant no harm.

"Yep, he's already getting belligerent. Hurry it up!" He yelled back in response to my attempt at peacemaking. This just confused me further. Why wouldn't he listen to me? What did I do to make him so hostile?

"And you *boy*, be quiet before it gets ugly." He said as he turned and spoke to you with overwhelming amounts of animosity.

"So you're really not going to even tell us what this is about? That's B.S.! You can't do this! You can't arrest us like this! That's against the law officer!" Shouted my brother who was also out of the car by now.

"Well why don't you shut up!" The officer shouted back. By that time, his partner, Eric, was there now with handcuffs out.

"Why don't you learn how to do your job!" Jaheem retorted. Damn, I wish he wouldn't make this so difficult. The officer was already hostile, he didn't have to antagonize him.

"That's it! Cuff 'em Eric!" Orders the officer to his partner Eric. "I got this one!" Eric sighed and went and marched towards Jaheem, fully prepared to restrain him. Suddenly the unnamed officer grabbed me by the back of the head and slammed me hard against my own car, denting it.

"Don't struggle or I'll clean your clock *boy!*" He whispered harshly. This was ridiculous. I wasn't even struggling! Now my head was pounding, I was about to be arrested, and I STILL don't know why I was pulled over. I thus let out my frustrations.

"Damn man! I'm not resisting, you don't have to attack me!" I exclaimed.

"Shut up!" Was all he said as he grabbed my arm roughly. He then grabbed my other arm and began putting them behind my back in an attempt to arrest me. Meanwhile, his partner Eric was trying to do the same with my brother with much less success. Jaheem kept pulling away and yanking his arm from the officer's grasp.

"Get your hands off me!" Yelled Jaheem after his latest act of defiance.

"Stop Resisting!" Shouted the officer, getting visibly angry at my brother's unwillingness to listen to orders. I didn't want anything worse to happen so I backed up the other's words, trying to get my brother to calm down.

"Jaheem! Stop! Just stop, we'll be fine." I tried to reassure him. Unfortunately he continued on as if he didn't hear a word I or the officer said and pushed the officer off of him.

"That's it!" Exclaims the officer, Eric, as he grabbed my 14 year old brother and slammed him hard against the car, as the other officer had done me. Knowing Jaheem, that only fired him up more, causing him to struggle with more intensity. The cop didn't let up and this time took out his taser and shocked Jabari, sticking him in the ribs with it. Jaheem still struggled, nearly getting loose so the cop tazed him again.

This still doesn't stop Jaheem from struggling out of his grasp, so Eric, the cop, takes out his night stick and begins beating Jaheem over the head and the ribs with it. THWACK THWACK THWACK, the cop hit him repeatedly, indiscriminately, and viciously, as he tried to put Jaheem down and beat the fight out of him.

At this point I too started to struggle. He had no reason to beat Jaheem like that! We did nothing wrong and were being wrongly arrested in the first place. He didn't strike the officer and did nothing to warrant repeated tazing and a beating of that nature. The first officer held me in place firmly, just gazing at the scene before him. Agitated I lashed out at him verbally.

"Hey! Get your partner under control! That's entirely uncalled for! He's a 14 year old boy!" I spat at the cop. He just laughed joyous and hearty laugh, an arrogant laugh, a laugh of derision.

11

"He should stop struggling then if he doesn't want to get beat. This is a good lesson for him. And for you." He added as an afterthought. "Keep that boy, that beast, under control, and maybe next time we'll only taze him once and give 'em a light beating." He finished with a slight chuckle.

I watched on as his partner Eric kept up the beating, at this point Jabari could only put his hands up to try and soften the blows. I had had enough, so I maneuvered my way out of the first officer's grasp and rushed to my brother's aid. Swiftly I pushed the cop off of him, stopping the beating in its tracks. Both cops looked on in awe and wonder, surprised at my actions, before Eric regained his lack-of-senses and swung the night stick at me this time.

Given that I was an athlete with quicker reaction speed than most, the night stick didn't even touch me as I easily moved out of the way and threw the cop backwards away from me and my brother. That didn't stop him for long as he was charging back in, this time with a taser. He swung the taser at my ribs, but I dodged that as well. He then swung with his night stick and I blocked it, taking it from his grasp. Finally I was hit by the taser at long range, and then punched in the jaw by the enraged officer. I stumbled back a bit before rushing forward, tackling the officer viciously (his head hitting the pavement), and laying him out with 2 punches (right straights).

Suddenly I came back to my senses and realized what I had done. I had just assaulted an officer of the law, and no matter the excuse I gave, the courts wouldn't be forgiving. I didn't regret it, as I'd be damned before letting my brother get beat like that in front of me, but it was time to give myself up and surrender. I didn't want to escalate this further.

I got up from the scuffle with my hands held high in the air and screamed "I surrender." It didn't seem to matter. The first cop that I escaped from, so that I could help Jaheem, had been watching the fight the entire time. When I won he apparently didn't like that and was going to put me down.

"Jabari he's got his gun out!" Yelled my brother, pointing to the still conscious officer. Sure enough he was right and the officer had pulled his gun and was pointing it, aiming it, and ready to shoot.

I managed to move right as the cop shot my way, the bullets hitting his partner Eric instead, presumably killing him on the spot. Panicked and flustered I scrambled on my hands and feet to get behind my car, shots ringing behind me as I moved. This was completely surreal, a cop shooting at me like some kind of criminal, and I still didn't know why I was being arrested. I mean...I was being shot at! This wasn't supposed to happen now or ever in my life! Yet here I was, racing away from a handful of bullets being fired in my direction. Even worse, the cop seemed to have gone rabid as he just shot and killed his partner! Before I could think any further, two more shots rang on my car, signaling to me that it was time to move.

I ran around my car as fast I could, not wanting the cop to get sight of me for that could equal death. I reached the cop's car in seconds, panting not from exhaustion but from the sheer craziness and mayhem around me. Taking a deep breath I ran once more, around the cop car this time and met face to face with my attempted shooter.

Immediately I rush him, grabbing his left arm and his right wrist, trying to get the gun out of his hands. I was stronger, but the officer had better leverage as I was still off balance from trying to escape certain death. For what seems like hours, but is certainly only a minute at best, we struggled back and forth until ultimately my strength prevailed. Unfortunately, the little advantage I got must have startled the cop and he tried to pull the trigger to shoot me off of him so he could finish me off. Seeing this, I quickly pointed the gun away from me and my brother and towards the officer himself.

BANG went the shot, through the officer's head as he fell to the floor, no longer breathing. I could only sit there in absolute shock as it happens.

Chapter 3: Realization

'I...I just killed a cop. Oh shit! I just killed a cop. They'll never let me out of prison for this. I'll never see Mom and Dad again, or any of my friends, and I'm sure as hell not going to college anymore. Speaking of Mom and Dad, they'll be devastated, disappointed in me to the highest level, and Jaheem's probably done too. I've ruined not just my own life, but his as well, as they'll say he's an accomplice. He'll never get to grow up normal, but in juvy (juvenile detention) if he's lucky, but probably in prison knowing the court system. Wait, Jaheem!' I thought as I snapped back to my senses.

"H-heem, you ok?" I asked timidly, still shaken up by the events that just transpired.

"Yeah I'm good. You?" He responded quickly. Oddly enough, despite being the younger brother, he seemed to handle himself better than I did. I don't know if maybe he somehow expected this or was putting on some type of façade, but I appreciated his strength.

"Yeah, I'm fine." I replied back quietly with a nod. Jaheem met my nod and looked around at the death, the carnage, the scene before us.

"So what do we do now?" He asked.

"I...I don't know. But we have to run." I replied truthfully.

"Should we drive home maybe? Mom and Dad might be able to help—" My little brother began.

"No! We don't want to get them in trouble too." I said, cutting him off. "Plus it'll make it easier to find us. We're now wanted men, killers, and there's not much they won't do to get us, maybe even to kill us..." I continued, trailing off at the end at the very thought of the cops, the city wanting us dead. It was terrifying to say the least. I really didn't know what to do in this situation. I never prepared for it or even thought about it. Being falsely and unfairly arrested didn't cross my mind much. Having cops beat my brother and taze him repeatedly even less so and...and killing cops isn't even something I ever fathomed doing under any circumstance. But here I am. No, here WE are, me and Jaheem against the world. On the run from the law.

"We need to lay low and hide the bodies, or else we'll be caught immediately." I finally finished after a long pause.

14

"Yeah...I get it. We can't contact anyone right now. It'll just mess both of us up. No matter who it is. And the bodies...I mean I've seen movies, I know how that goes." He said, as he got up and walked around. Unbeknownst to me at that time, he had gone to pick up their guns and tasers for safe keeping. I followed him a few minutes after, still in shock from the events that unfolded, to help with covering our tracks. Jaheem was busy struggling with Eric's body (the cop that was beating him and fought me) while I went and grabbed the first officer. The body was heavy and I only got it halfway before my arms got tired. I never thought something like 200 or so pounds would be so heavy, but I remembered the term 'dead weight' and how it was supposedly much heavier than normal weight. I definitely see what they mean now, it felt like 2-3x heavier than expected. Wiping sweat from my brow I saw that Jaheem was further behind than me, about 40% of the way to the car. At that moment I had a plan and relayed it to my brother.

"Yo 'Heem." I called out, with the body in my hands still, as I dragged it to the cop car, out of view of what I knew to be a camera on the windshield or near it. Jaheem was still struggling and barely spared a glance my way as he answered.

"What?" He gasped out, tired and agitated from the work.

"These dudes are heavy." I stated the obvious as I stopped my movements of dragging the officer to his car. Jaheem gave me a look that said 'you don't say' in response.

"Yeah so?" He asked, irritation coming through his voice.

"So...we should do them one at a time with both of us on one body. It'll be quicker that way." I explained to him. He looked down at the body and back up to me, down at the body and back up to me, before letting go of the body and shrugging.

"Yeah sure, makes sense to me." He replied as he walked over and grabbed the legs to help me pick up the body and move it twice as fast if not more. "So where we putting him?" He asked as we walked him over.

"The car." I answered obviously, a bit confused on the seemingly rhetorical question. He looked annoyed at my answer and asked again.

"Yeah but where? Front Seat? Back Seat? Trunk?" Oh, that's what he meant. Well the front seat was out due to the camera. Didn't want our movements caught on tape. The backseat was alright, but it'd raise questions as to why a cop was in the backseat of his own car. It might draw attention. If it were our car or my car it'd work, but that wasn't a choice, again due to the camera. So trunk it was.

"Trunk. We want to avoid the camera and avoid anyone seeing them just sitting there in the car. Trunk makes us look guiltier, but that only matters if we get caught. And we won't." I pointed out, explaining it to him. It seemed to make sense as 'Heem just nodded and continued helping me to carry the cop's body to the trunk. I manned the load as he opened the trunk, and then we threw him in there, careful not to close it yet. We had another body to move. I felt like a monster, a psychopath with how we were moving dead bodies, bodies of people we killed as far as the law was concerned. It bothered me more how quickly I thought of it and how calmly we were moving them. The second body, Eric's, was moved without much thought, struggle, or fanfare, and we got him to the trunk, put him on top of his partner, and closed it shut. I sat down with hands bloody (figuratively), hoping that somehow, some way no one heard the commotion (with the gunshots, the yelling, the slamming, the moving and shuffling of bodies and all types of loud activities) and that we were now safe for a while, at least long enough to escape. For now we were good and had hidden what we'd done.

So what now? We're wanted fugitives but there might be a chance that the news hadn't broken the story just yet. We're probably going to want something to eat and drink too: snacks, water, juice, dinner, all the good stuff. After that, I don't know, we'll wing it or something. With my realization, I got up off of the floor and wiped my hands on my pants, brushing myself off. I looked around and didn't see anybody. The streets were conveniently empty and no one was around or outside at all. My prayers had been answered and there were no witnesses, which was good, heaven sent even. I didn't think I'd have the heart to 'get rid' of them, so we'd probably be caught immediately if there were any. Knowing the coast was clear, I turned to my brother to see if he was down with the plan.

"Yo 'Heem." I started, just trying to get his attention.

"Yeah, bro?" He asked, his head turning towards me, as if I distracted him from something.

"So I was thinking...we're wanted men, killers even, but right now no one knows that. We need food, we need water, something to drink, and I think we should take advantage of this time while we can. After this, cops will probably be all over us and we won't be able to go anywhere without being run down by police." I explained my plans and my feelings to him.

He looked contemplative, as if he was running through my logic, and he probably was. After a few more seconds he replied.

"It makes sense. I'm down. Let's hurry though; I'm not trying to go to jail."

With that decided, we got back in my car, in spite of the cameras, and drove, looking for a place to eat. We didn't want fast food as that never lasted long, we'd just be hungry an hour later, so we were looking for a restaurant or a place where we could sit down and enjoy a good meal. Initially I wanted just a grocery store type place, where we could stop and shop in peace, but Jaheem insisted we make the most of it and go to a restaurant.

"Come on bruh, we won't have another chance to do this. Once they know, once they start searching for us, we're done. Let's enjoy it while we can." He spoke, voicing his logic.

It was risky, but now was the only time we could feasibly take that risk and we weren't exactly thinking straight, still in shock from having our lives flipped upside down. We drove for no longer than 10 minutes before we finally decided on a barbecue grill to stop and eat at. I parked my car as close as possible and we stepped out, ready for our last meal, so to speak. The whole time we kept looking around our shoulders as we walked, wary of someone somehow knowing about us and what we've done. It was highly unlikely, but still a possibility and we really couldn't stop ourselves. During the walk the sun all eyes seemed to be on us and I started getting nervous and doubting our judgment, doubting our decision to sit down and eat.

'Murder and nerves makes the body hunger, so of course it's perfect time to eat!' I thought to myself sarcastically, steadily questioning everything we were doing. When we walked, we didn't really pass many people, a man here, a woman there, a group of children etc. The lot and the restaurant weren't empty, but they were far from crowded thankfully. We had to have been walking slow as hell and looking all types of suspicious, but no one really paid us attention. We were lucky. And even then, despite our luck, we were still very aware, too aware of our surroundings. Even when we walked in and talked to the patron, we gave a fake name to eat under and constantly looked behind and around us.

The wait was 15 minutes, not too long in a normal situation, but not fast enough for us as we were in a hurry and literally on the run. The entire time we sat in the waiting room, legs constantly in movement, shaking, as our heads moved on a swivel. The red interior of the restaurant constantly passed our eyes in a blur, as did the wood of the furniture. The people there seemed happy, jovial, they didn't know about us. It seemed we were safe. Finally, the fake name was called and we got up silently, walked a few feet, sat down, and looked over the menu. It only took us a few minutes before we realized that we had to discuss the plan for payment.

"So...are we paying or we dashing? I need to know how much to order." Asks Jaheem.

"We're paying. So just get a normal meal. What kind of cash you got on you?" I replied, finishing my statement with a question. Jaheem looked down, hands ruffling through his pockets, before answering.

"I only got like $20 left after buying snacks and stuff. I think we're going to have to dash or get REALLY cheap meals." He said. I mirrored his actions, and saw that I only had around $30 in my pockets. So 'Heem was

17

right. We couldn't pay unless we got cheap meals. Well, maybe we can. Just avoid steak and anything like that, get water for drinks, and we should be good. I relay this message to my brother.

"I only got $30. But we can still pay. Just don't get anything expensive like steak. Get a burger. And get water for a drink, and we can do this." I said. My brother's face scrunched up at my statement, but he then thought about it, and his face calmed down and he seemed to agree. He didn't voice it though, he only nodded as we sat there, waiting for the server to come to us.

We waited in silence, knowing damn well that we can't say anything here for fear of someone overhearing. So it was silence or small talk. Given what just happened, we definitely didn't want to talk about something so trivial. So silence it was.

It took another 5 minutes before the server came, a young white woman around 19-22 years old, with brown hair tied into a bun. She was of course wearing the standard waitress uniform of a red dress with a black apron and her name tag on her left side. Jenna.

"How are y'all doing today?" She asked with bright eyes and a happy demeanor.

"Fine." Replied my brother, sounding bored.

"We're good." Was my statement. Short and to the point. Didn't feel like talking much given what just happened.

"That's good. My name is Jenna and I'll be serving you today. Can I ask what you want to drink?" She asked, readying her pen, to write down our orders. Jaheem opened his mouth as if to order something else, but then remembered what we discussed and closed it, swallowing his words. He prepared himself and finally spoke.

"Water please." He said quietly.

"OK, and you sir?" She said, turning to me after writing down Jaheem's order of water.

"Same. Water for me too." I said.

"OK, well I'll go get your drinks and then come back and see if you're ready to order." She replied, putting her pen and pad down and heading off to get our water.

5 more minutes of silence passed before she came back with 2 glasses of water, 2 straws, and a basket full of garlic toast. She handed each of us a glass and a straw, and placed the basket in the middle of the table.

She then got out her pen and pad and prepared to take our orders for our meals.

"Hello y'all, are y'all ready to order?" She inquired. We both looked at each other, and silently communicated. Yes, we were both ready to order. We both nodded and replied with a "yes."

"OK, so who's going first?" She asked earnestly. I shrugged and Jaheem took that as confirmation to start his order.

'I'll go first." He said, before looking down at his menu. "I'll get the basic burger. Fries for the side."

"OK, and what'll you have?" She questioned, turning to me.

"I'll get barbecue chicken fingers." I said, closing my menu. I was more relaxed, calm. This was more like real life and less like the surreal new life we had just carved out for ourselves, so I was more at ease in this world, even when realistically I should've been more frantic and alert than ever.

"And what do you want for the side?" She asked, snapping me out of my thoughts.

"Fries." I answered quickly.

"Soup or Salad?"

"Salad." Apparently one word answers were my new specialty.

"OK, that's all I need. Your food will be out in a moment." Again she left, and this time it took her 20 minutes to return with 2 plates of food in hand. During the wait, we staved off the silence by eating the 3 pieces of garlic toast. Each of us claiming 1 and a half pieces. The biting and chewing wasn't obnoxious, but compared to the silence from before, it was thundering. I liked it. Silence was boring, albeit somewhat necessary. That only took a few moments so we spent the rest of it just...staring, observing, and looking around the room and such. I was deep in my thoughts, mentally sizing up each person, judging mainly three things about them: how likely they were to see us, how likely they were to remember us, and how likely they were to report us to police if asked. Some I mentally assigned the role of 'snitch' or 'teller', a person who wouldn't wait for police to ask them, but would make it their business to rat us out. There only a few of these people, scattered throughout the restaurant, but their presence made me nervous, even if it was made up and fictitious in every form and fashion. If I thought about it, almost everyone here would fall into my first 2 categories of people. Me and my brother weren't exactly inconspicuous. Being black males automatically made certain people notice us and be wary, and my afro and his braids didn't help us to blend in at all. Everyone remembers the guys with unique hair, especially when they were together. Basically we were doomed If anyone here was asked about us. 20 minutes passed by quickly with these kind of thoughts, and before I knew it, our waitress was here with our food.

Once we received our food, we dug in, drinking our half full glasses of water (some of it drunk from when we were eating toast) every so often, and generally just enjoying our food, my previous thoughts all but forgotten. The server forgot my salad, but I didn't bring it to attention. The last thing I wanted was extra attention. 'Heem noticed too and smirked a bit at me, before digging into his burger, taking another huge bite. 'Heem finished before me and had to wait for a few minutes as I finished picking at my fries. Finally we were done. We got up to go quietly as we could, like ninjas, as we left $25 on the table to pay for our food. As soon as we left, I addressed my brother after coming to a conclusion.

"Yeah we can't do that again." I said, as we got to the car, thankfully unbothered by anyone. Jaheem raised an eyebrow in response.

"What?"

"Going to a restaurant, or any public place like that where we're enclosed in a tight space and forced to wait." I explained in simple terms. Jaheem's eyes filled with realization as he nodded slowly and reached the same conclusion I had, that we had been lucky that this went so well for us.

"Yeah, I see it now. If anyone came to get us, we'd be done. We're already waiting so that wouldn't seem strange if the waitress did anything like talk to the cops or turn us in, and if they came after us we only got like 2 places to run to. And both are mad easy to cut off. On top of that, unless we sit in a specifically strategic spot, we can't see anyone come and go with any kind of needed accuracy, and could be surprised at any moment." He said, fully showing his understanding and voicing the main issues with doing something like that again. I just nodded as he went into detail as to why what we did was so dumb and risky. I was almost surprised, but then I remembered that 'Heem had always been a smart kid, even if he was impulsive and aggressive at times. He was my brother after all. After that diatribe, we were both in the car, buckled up and ready to go. We had gotten food, no matter how foolishly we'd done it, so now we had to move on to the next thing: water.

We drove to the closest grocery store and parked, getting out to walk into the store, just like at the restaurant. Before we walked in, I put my hand on 'Heem's chest, stopping his movement. He looked at me questioningly, so I spoke, voicing my current thoughts.

"We need water for a long time, but we can't just lug around entire packages of water. I say we get 2 large water bottles, each with a purifier. This way we can carry a good amount of water, and get it from anywhere." I explained. He thought about it and nodded slowly.

"Makes sense. Now get your hand off my chest and let's go." He said, walking forward into the store as I obliged. I sighed and followed him in, still speaking.

"Remember, we also need food. Food we can eat at any moment and that won't spoil. So no cans or anything we need to cook. Whenever this...search starts, we probably won't have access to anything close to an oven or anything that can cook food. And we're not breaking in anywhere. It's too risky."

"Alright so basically we're getting water bottles, bread, apples, peanut butter, and...a knife for the peanut butter I guess." He answered me.

"Yeah, sounds like a good start. But you sure you want peanut butter with a limited supply of water? We all know you need some kind of liquid to wash down something so...dense." I replied, avoiding saying the word 'thick' for obvious reasons.

"Yeah. I like peanut butter. And it's filling. Plus it's something to put on the bread." He explained as we traversed the store. Instantly I spotted the water bottles, looking closely to see if I could find one with a purifier on it. There were ones with twisting tops, ones with tops that just popped up, and ones with tops that twisted but were still attached. Unfortunately, none of them had purifiers on them. There wasn't anything here. Damn. We needed a bigger store, maybe a hardware store or a supermarket, something with a camping section more than likely. Looks like that was our next stop.

Oh well, in the mean time we could still get bread, apples, and...peanut butter apparently, from this store. I looked around and saw that my brother had already gotten the peanut butter and bread, so I walked over to the fresh fruit section and picked out 3 bags of apples and took them to the front. I waited for what seemed a minute or so until Jaheem finally made it up front with a giant jar of peanut butter and a huge loaf of potato bread. I shook my head at the excess, but knew that we might need to shop in such a way, as once we're discovered...well it was probably over as far as shopping goes. I quickly paid for the purchase, got a bag for our groceries and hurried Jaheem out of the store.

He quickly looked through the bag and his face scrunched up once he saw what was there.

"Hey man, where's the water?" He asked. I could only sigh at his question.

"There weren't any bottles that had purifiers in them. Not at that store. We need to find a bigger store, a supermarket of some kind, and try the camping section." I informed him.

"Camping?" He asked, taken aback.

"Yeah, camping. Campers are the most likely to need those kind of water bottles, so it'd only make sense that it's in the camping section." I explained.

"I guess. " Is all he said as we quietly got back in the car and drove, on our way to the megastore supermarket we needed. It was a ways off, and we had to go through a bit of traffic to get there unfortunately. It turned a 5 minute drive into a 20 minute one.

Finally we arrived at the Big Mart, the large red themed store that had all of our (and anyone else's if you let them tell it) needs. The sliding doors part automatically as we step inside, welcoming us to enter, to buy, to spend. I stopped and stared for a second at just how large this store was, not because I hadn't shopped there before or because I wasn't used to it, but because of our current situation as fugitives. Would it be beneficial to us to be in such a large store should someone get word of us and what we did? On one hand, we would have plenty of space to run, plenty of exits to escape through, and it'd be hard to pinpoint us in the sea of people currently perusing through the megastore. On the other hand, the bigger the store usually meant the bigger the security measures and we could easily be caught on camera or be blocked by a large mass of people or authorities, preventing us from escaping. I shook those thoughts from my head. Either way, that didn't matter. For now we were undiscovered. For now we were safe. Now let's find that camping section.

I turned to my brother and shook my head "no" when he looked to get a shopping cart to aid us in our search. It might sound paranoid, but I didn't want ANYTHING drawing extra attention to us nor did I want something that could slow us down. If the water bottles were in our hand, we could easily run and make a break for it. If they're in the basket, we either run without them and lose a valuable piece of equipment needed for our survival, or we have to waste precious time by retrieving it from said basket. That time could lead to us being shot, tazed, or subdued in some other way. No way would I risk that.

With a wave of my hand I beckoned Jaheem to follow me, as we searched for the ever allusive water bottles with purifiers in them. We started by basically staring at the signs, looking for the camping section, but eventually noticed how strange we looked, so we opted to glancing at the signs above the aisles ever so slightly as we passed. Clothing, Games, Cookies, Chips, Spices, Bread, Snacks, Vitamins, Medical, Sports etc. we passed by almost every aisle in the store before we finally found what we came here for, the camping section. Hurriedly we stepped inside the aisle, scanning it quickly with our eyes. It seemed as if we were out of luck, when we got to the end of the aisle. There it-- no, there *they* were, water bottles with filters in them. They weren't purifiers, but they were just as good. I quickly snatched up two of them, 21 oz each and my face fell when I looked at the price tags. Each of them were $50 a piece and on sale at that. We couldn't afford that.

22

We'd have to steal them.

With a deep breath I spoke to 'Heem to relay the message.

"Jaheem, we can't buy these. They're too expensive. We'll have to come back later." I said while glancing down. My statement only served to confuse him.

"Come back later? Jabari, did you forget something? We can't exactly waltz in here at any time and just buy these with more money—oh. Oh, I see. Yeah, we'll have to come back later for them." He said, starting to rant, but realizing half way through what I meant. He then finished his statement with a cringe worthy wink.

"Yeah, don't do that." I said as I kept the bottle in my hand and walked off towards the exit. Now how were we going to do this? As I said before, bigger stores had bigger and better security, and this was the biggest store there was. I imagine that the sensors will go off as soon as we get near them and then BOOM we're caught. From there we get held, our true crime gets discovered, we go to trial, and then to prison for life, if not the death penalty. Okay, maybe I was going overboard, but it was a possibility. We had to make a plan.

"Jaheem." I whispered, trying to get his attention. Unfortunately he ignored me. "Jaheem." I tried again.

"What?" He whispered back, hearing me the second time.

"We have to come up with a plan to get these bottles out. Got any ideas?" I asked.

"How are you going to say we need a plan and not have a plan yourself?" He furiously whispered back, a bit bewildered.

"I don't know, I'm thinking. Just trying to see if maybe you had something in mind." I told him truthfully.

"Yeah, you distract the person by asking where the bathroom is, just as someone else walks out. I slide the bottle through the sensors when they walk through and the person will stop them. Then we just walk through and pick up the bottles." He whispered without hesitation.

"That sounds dangerous, risky. What if you get caught sliding them?" I asked, still in a whisper, concerned about the very same consequences I had thought about earlier. Getting caught was not an option.

"Then I run. We can't get caught. You know that. So we got to do what we got to do." He whispered back with finality.

"Fine. Just don't mess up." I whispered back, ending the discussion. He nodded in affirmation but rolled his eyes afterwards, showing his exasperation with my caution. I let it slide. It's not like I could scold him right now, we were nearly at the exit. Me and him separated immediately, me looking at clothes, and him looking at snacks to prepare for our roles.

It seemed like an hour before someone came, though it was likely only 5 minutes or so, and it was time to put our plan in action. As soon as they got close, I began walking towards the greeter. As soon as the greeter checked their receipt and gave them the go ahead, and I mean not even a half a second afterwards, I stepped up and asked them politely as I could where the bathroom was.

"The bathroom?" Began the old lady with a bit of a pause. She was dressed in the company shirt and had kind green eyes to go along with her short white hair, wrinkled skin, thin build, and short stature. "The bathroom is just down there, and take a left--" She almost finished, before the sensors beeped. She turned around slowly, and I was on my way towards the bathroom, to at least fake like my part was real. Glancing over, I saw her stop the previous customer, a middle aged blonde haired man with a stout build, a mustache, and a green shirt with khakis, and ask to look back over his receipt. As she did, Jaheem glanced over to me for a second before walking nonchalantly through the sensors to get our water.

Quickly I slid into the bathroom, washed my hands for some kind of proof, and then slid back out, eager to meet my brother outside of the store. Walking back the way I came, I nodded to the kind old lady as I exited the store, on the path to my brother. As expected, he was waiting for me right outside with a wide grin on his face.

"Told you it'd work." He said, still looking forward as we began our walk to the car.

"You did. Sorry I doubted you, oh wise one." I taunted him.

"Yeah, just make sure you don't do it again." He said. I could only roll my eyes at his arrogance. I then did a double take as I noticed something. The peanut butter, bread, apples, and the knife we got from before were gone. When did he have time to hide it? And where? How did I not think of that? Clearly we couldn't just bring it into another store like that with us. I opened my mouth to voice my questions, but he raised his hand to silence me as I did.

"Relax, Jabari. We're about to pass right by it. I left it somewhere safe." He said with confidence. I eyed him skeptically, but nodded and waited for him to show me exactly what he meant. We went in a different direction than the car, walking past the parking lot and the building itself. A few more minutes and we passed an old blue mail letter box that he reached into and pulled out our previous groceries. I didn't know if it was a genius move or completely stupid so I just said nothing and shook my head and kept walking. It was strange however, as I didn't quite know where we were walking to at the moment. At some point in time we would be discovered, our crime would at least, so it'd be best to start heading to a destination of some sort. Jaheem thought the same thing.

"Ay yo, where are we going? Shouldn't we be trying to escape rather than just wandering around, waiting to be caught? I don't know about you bruh, but I'm not trying to go to jail." He blurted out. He was right; we should have a destination in mind, but...where? I mean we're wanted killers, so nowhere in the country was safe.

"I...I don't know." I confessed, answering my brother's question.

"What?" He asked, confused at my lack of plan. I answered again with a shrug.

"I don't know. I can't think of anywhere in the country that's safe 'Heem. We're wanted killers, or we're going to be. No one's going to take us in. Nowhere is a good place to go." I explained to him.

"Yeah...that's why we should leave the country." He replied.

"What?" This time it was my turn to be confused, bewildered at his response.

"You said it yourself, you can't think of anywhere in the country that's safe. Keyword, *in this country*. So we leave. We're in Texas, it can't be too far off, I mean we're practically already in Mexico. From there we can get away and avoid the law. Get somewhere *safe*." He continued, describing his train of thought to me.

"Yeah but...what about our parents?" I asked. "Our friends, our family, would everyone know what happened? What would they think about this? I'd rather let them know where we're going and what the deal is before just up and leaving. I can't have Moms looking at me like a cold-blooded killer. I just can't."

Jaheem shakes his head at my thoughts and sighs.

"That's how people get caught Jabari. Haven't you seen any movies? The less people that know, the better." Was his reply. Again he was right, telling everyone would put both us and them in more danger than necessary. But still, I meant what I said. I had to at least clear the air with our parents. I can't live with being a murderer in their eyes.

"Okay, so we don't tell everyone, but we still got to tell Mom and Dad. I meant what I said before about how they view us. I can't do it. All it is is one call." I pleaded after deliberating with myself. Jaheem seemed to mutter under his breath in frustration, almost as if talking to himself. After the self-talk was over, he looked up

25

at me.

"Alright bro, you got it. Just Mom and Dad though. No one else. Then we start making our way to the border, to the Promise Land." He decided. "Never thought I'd call Mexico of all places the Promise Land." He added on under his breath.

"Yeah 'cause that's the craziest thing that's happened today. Not…anything else that we did or anything else that happened to us. It's Mexico being the Promise Land." I replied sarcastically, leaving out the details in case anyone was listening in. My brother just gave me a look before responding.

"What? You salty 'cause you can't call your girl or something? And yeah, that's still crazier than anything else that's happened. Mexico is just…the opposite of the Promise Land. And you know it." He spat back at me. Speaking of salty, it seemed like he needed a tall glass of water himself. I just can't believe that out of being pulled over for no reason, which escalated further to a cop killing his own partner, and then me accidentally killing that cop which forced us on the run, the craziest thing to 'Heem is Mexico being a Promise Land. I think he's just too afraid to admit he's wrong.

"Nah, I can't agree with that one. But whatever, let's move on and find a payphone, so they can't trace us with the call." His face lit up at that statement.

"Oh, so you *do* watch movies! Good. That'll make this easier." He spoke with approval.

"Cool, but…how are we going to find a pay phone exactly?" I questioned, genuinely concerned with how to possibly locate one without incriminating ourselves or allowing ourselves to be caught. He just looked at me and shrugged as he took out his cellphone and began typing. He continued typing in it, hit a button, typed again, hit another button, and then brought it up to show it to me.

"It's here." He said, showing me his phone's screen. I only raised my eyebrow at his actions.

"Won't using our cellphones make us easily traceable?" I inquired, pretty sure I heard that in both life and in the movies.

"Nah. I mean, yeah it will, but it's more about even having our cellphones. The GPS in them is traceable, and I don't know how to stop that so…"He trailed off.

"So…?" I asked, waiting for him to finish.

"So we're probably going to have to get rid of them right after this call anyways or we'll be found out. So no harm in using them one last time, know what I mean?" Was his reply.

26

"I guess. It makes sense." I replied. "But then why wouldn't we just use our cellphones to call Mom and Dad?" I finished with a question. Seriously, it'd be a lot easier than going all the way to a payphone just to talk to them, when we had our cellphones on us already.

"Because..." He seemed to trail off, trying to think of something. As I thought, there wasn't a good reason. My mouth formed into a smirk as I watched him struggle.

"Because...it's good practice." He said lamely. I opened my mouth to speak as if to say 'Really? That's the best you could do?', but he cut me off before I could.

"And if they look at their phone records, Mom and Dad, then they can tell we called. Not definitively. I mean, they might be able to trace it to this payphone, but whatever, that's not concrete. But from our cellphones? That's an open and shut case." He finished smugly. I have to admit, it was a really good point. There was nothing I could say to refute it. He stared at me expectantly, waiting for a response. I just put my hands up in surrender.

"You got it 'Heem, you got it." Was all I could say as I accepted defeat; from my little brother of all people.

And so we took off, following the directions 'Heem looked up on his phone, to find the nearest payphone. It was about a block away, so we didn't have to walk far, just go straight, cross to the other side of the street, and then turn left. Sure enough, true to his phone, there it was: Salvation. Well maybe not salvation, but it was at least communication with our family. It was reassurance, that our parents wouldn't see us as monsters and as murderers. It was the comfort of hearing their voices again and not leaving them to worry about our whereabouts and about the real story, what REALLY happened when the cops attacked me and 'Heem and basically forced the kill. All of these were wrapped up in one little package with a metaphorical red bow on top. I could only stare in silence at the payphone for the first ten seconds, but eventually gathered my wits.

Exchanging a look with my brother, I grabbed the phone with shaky hands and dialed my parents' number, the home phone. The phone rang once as my heart thumped wildly and rapidly as nervousness overtook me. The phone rang again as my hands got sweaty and my throat got dry. This could and likely would be the last time talking to my parents in a long time, if not forever. The phone rang a third time and I patiently waited, sweating from my brow as suddenly I was very warm. It then rang again, the final ring on our home phone. Was everything alright? Had someone gotten to our parents? Did someone know? Did someone find out about us? Thoughts raced through my mind as the phone went back to dial tone and the call went unanswered. I had a worried look on my face, as my brother looked at me pointedly, literally pointed a finger at me and said one word.

27

"No!" He exclaimed as he shook his head. He didn't want to hear any of my paranoia and he could see it written across my face. For his sake I swallowed my words and relinquished the phone to him as he beckoned for it with his hand out. He swiftly grabbed it and dialed the same familiar number that I just did. I hoped he got a better response.

Jaheem seemed to handle the call better than I did. I don't know if it's him being too young to understand the gravity of the situation, of the conversation and the consequences of our actions, or if he was just more level headed than me. Or maybe he's just good at hiding it. Any of these were possibilities. He held the phone to his ear for about ten seconds, a little more, and it appeared he also got through the four rings with no answer. BANG! He suddenly slammed the phone onto the hook, anger apparent on his face, anger and worry.

"HNNG!" He grunted in frustration at getting no answer. All I could do was put my hand on his shoulder in an attempt to comfort him.

"Relax. They're fine." I spoke softly, not really believing the words myself. But it didn't really matter what I believed, I needed to calm 'Heem down. Acting irrationally can only end badly for us. Jaheem's head turned sharply towards me, whipping in anger as his eyes showed nothing but pure fury.

"How can you know that?! You're just...saying stuff!" He yelled at me, lashing out in fear and rage, scared of what may have happened to our parents. He was right though. I didn't know, and I was just saying stuff, but it's what we needed to believe. And I had to do something drastic to prove it.

"I just do." I said calmly, not falling into the trap of a yelling match with my little brother of all people. "Here, I'll prove it." I said as I moved past him, picked up the phone, and dialed the number once more. Internally I was sweating and incredibly nervous, hoping to God that my parents pick up this time and answer their phone. Maybe they thought we were spam, or telemarketers, or just didn't answer since they didn't know the number? Surely by the third time they would at least be curious enough to answer? There was only one way to find out, and I was already halfway through that solution. It rang once, then twice, then a third time. No answer. However, before the fourth ring a magical and wondrous thing happened. Someone picked up and answered.

"Hello –" I began to say, but was immediately cut off by the angry ranting of my dad. Jaheem's head whipped up and towards me in shock, having previously fallen as he looked to the ground, downtrodden due to his negative, albeit realistic thoughts.

"Who is this, and why do you keep calling my number!?" He asked with a raised voice.

"Dad it's me." I answered quickly and excitedly. His voice then changed to one of realization and confusion.

"Jabari? Why are you calling us from some strange number? You're not in jail are you? Is this your 'one phone call'?" He inquired in an annoyed tone.

"No Dad, I'm not in jail. And I'm calling from this number because...because we're in trouble." I responded, hesitating to truly tell my parents how much trouble we were in.

"In trouble? What do you mean in trouble? What—"

"Dad we killed a cop." I paused and took a deep breath, taking in the silence on the other end, no doubt due to the shock my dad was experiencing at the moment. "*I* killed a cop. We were coming back from the store when we were suddenly pulled over for no reason. They...the cop was very rude, talking down to us, and seemed to be jumpy and paranoid, always grabbing on his gun." I began weaving the tale from memory.

"So you killed him!" Shouted Dad from the other side of the phone.

"No. Well...yeah, but not because of that. He started to arrest us, also for no reason, and called his partner for backup. Both of them were rough, the first cop on me, the second cop on Jaheem, and...and...well Jaheem kept fighting back. Even before this he was trading words with the first cop. I tried to calm him down, but you know how he is." I stopped again to swallow some spit. My throat got dry and formed a lump as I thought about what happened next. "Like I said, the cops were rough and Jaheem was fighting back. So the second cop started tazing him and beating him, and...and I asked him to stop, pleaded with him, but he kept going. I just snapped."

"And that's when you killed him?" Asked my dad in a low and soft voice. I shook my head in refutation, despite him not being able to see me.

"No. I...I attacked him. We fought for a while, I won and knocked him out—"

"You fought a cop? What were you *thinking*?" He interrupted before I could get out more of the story.

"I was *thinking* about protecting my little brother. I'm not going to let anyone just beat on him like that! Not even a cop!" I lashed out, not wanting to be criticized for simply defending my brother. That was my job, to defend him. No matter what anyone said, even my own dad. "*Anyways*," I started, voicing my annoyance, "we fought, I won and knocked him out. The other cop, the first cop, had brought out his gun for whatever reason." I explained.

"He brought out his *gun*? Are you serious? What was he trying to kill you? This is unacceptable! I'll call the Police Chief myself and get this straightened out!" Yelled my dad in outrage.

"Wait...just wait before you do that." I responded in a soft voice. "Something happened and..." I stopped to take a gulp. "If you call the Police Chief, We'll be going to prison. Forever. Remember Dad, we killed a *cop*. Even if it's self-defense, they're not letting us off." I pause for a few seconds, waiting for confirmation from my Dad. He says nothing and remains silent.

"So...so he brought out a gun, but I didn't see it. Jaheem warned me and I had to duck and dodge shots, moving left and right and right and left. Finally I got to him and tried to wrestle the gun out of his hand, disarm him you know, but I couldn't. It...it ended up with the gun going off on his face, killing him. And before that, he shot his partner when trying to kill me, so we look like bonafide cop killers. So we ran. We just wanted you to know the real story and not whatever they say on the media when they paint us as bloodthirsty killers."

"I see... Thank you for that son. Your mother would be heartbroken if she didn't know the truth. But don't get me wrong, she wouldn't believe the media. And neither would I. Now is there anything else you want to tell us?" He replied, asking with a softer tone. I looked around at Jaheem and took another deep breath. I suppose it'd be best to tell them about our plans. It'd screw up plausible deniability, but they needed to know where we were going and that we were safe.

"Actually yeah. Me and Jaheem...we plan on leaving."

"Leaving?" Asked Dad in a surprised tone, taken aback at my statement.

"Escaping. Going to the border and probably over to Mexico where we won't go to prison hopefully. I'm not sure I should be telling you this, plausible deniability and all of that, but I didn't want you guys to worry any more than you have to, being parents and all." I explained, my words getting faster as I got more and more nervous.

"Jabari, you don't have to do this. We can fight this! Run prints on the gun! Get testimony from witnesses! From the police car camera! Anything other than simply leaving. Your mother...your mother will be devastated." He replied, trying to get me to see reason. Unfortunately I couldn't be persuaded. I knew that nothing he said would work. I had touched the murder weapon personally, so the prints wouldn't work. I didn't see any witnesses around when everything went down, and even if there were, witnesses can easily be threatened and coerced into doing anything the police wanted. They were far more powerful than two random black teenage males. And the police camera, well no matter what it had on it, even if against all odds it caught the entire thing, we would still go to prison for some kind of murder case. And that just wasn't acceptable to me.

"Dad, we do have to do this. Those ideas won't work. I can get into detail, but I don't really want to. Just...trust me, they won't work." I pleaded with my dad to see reason, reversing our roles. There was silence on the phone, as if he was thinking on my words. I took another gulp and continued on with more of our plans.

"So back to the plausible deniability. That's actually why we're calling you from this phone. Jaheem had the idea to not use our cellphones so you can say that you've had no contact with us. This keeps you guys out of harm's way. We're even going to get rid of our cellphones so they can't track us with the GPS inside, so don't bother calling us and making yourself worry. Just...trust us. We'll be fine. I promise." I said, letting it all out in one breath. Still he was silent. "Is...is Mom there? Can I speak with her? This is the...the last time we'll be able to really contact you guys until we get over the border, and I...I don't know I just want to speak with her." More silence. Finally after around five seconds, replied in a low voice.

"I think it's best to leave your mom out of this. I'll tell her what you said." I...that was unacceptable. I get where he's coming from, but I just wanted to speak to her one last time. Contrary to what I said before, this might be the last time we speak to her ever, not just when we get over the border. I just wanted to say some last words.

"Dad, please. I just need to say some last words." I pleaded in a desperate voice. He sighed into the phone and I heard some rumbling that indicated movement. Some voices could be heard in the background, one female (Mom), and one male (Dad). Finally the phone picked back up and Mom's voice filled my ears.

"Honey, 'Bari, how is my baby? What's this your father says about you being in trouble? Is Jaheem with you? Is he alright? When are you coming home, you've been gone for hours!? Why are you calling from a strange phone? What—" Mom ranted on, asking question after question and not allowing any time to answer them.

"Mom? Mom!" I interrupted her. "Calm down. I'm fine, Jaheem's fine and yes he's with me. We're in serious trouble and that's why we're calling from this phone and also why..." I trailed off not sure how to say it.

"Why what, baby?" She asked in a way only a mother can.

"Why we won't be coming back home." I finished in a low voice. "Before you say anything, me and 'Heem are in big trouble for a bad crime, so we go back home, we get arrested and thrown in jail. I don't want to go to jail, and I don't want 'Heem to grow old in there either." I explained, cutting her off before she could voice her outrage. It was her turn to be silent now for a few seconds.

"So what do you plan on doing?" She asked softly, seemingly understanding the situation a lot more than Dad did.

"We, um, we plan on leaving the country, hopping the border so we can't be arrested." I replied.

"And Jaheem is OK with this plan?" She inquired. I almost laughed since it was his idea in the first place.

"Yeah, he thought of it in the first place." I informed her. I almost slapped my head as I realized my mistake too late.

"And you're going to listen to your fourteen year old brother? Are you hearing yourself Jabari!?" She yelled in rage.

"Yes Mom, I am. It makes sense, it's a good idea, and as much as it pains me to say, he's right. I'm sorry." She's silent once more. Likely making a face of anger and slowly accepting our decision.

"It's that bad then?" She asked quietly. I nodded even though she couldn't see me.

"Yeah it's that bad." I said.

"Oh, my poor boy! Well just know that Mommy loves you and you have my full support." She said in a sad and loving tone. Almost like she knew this might be the last time we speak. Ever.

"I do. And I love you too Mom." I responded with a shaky and emotional voice.

"Now let me speak to my youngest child." She requested. I could only nod and give Jaheem a look before passing the phone to him and exchanging places. I didn't look at him during my conversation with Mom and Dad, so I didn't see how he was taking it. From what I could see now, he looked a lot better than when he was raging over not being able to reach them. His mouth, his face said happy as he held a smile and his expression had brightened, but his eyes, his eyes said sad. Likely he was sad as this was the last time we'd be able to speak to our parents, just as I was, yet happy we could reach them and that he could get a chance to say something to them before we left on our journey to The Promise Land, Mexico. I was relieved once I got to talk to them and explain what was happening, so I was sure he'd feel the same once he was done, though he'd likely do far less explaining. I'd done enough for the both of us.

Jaheem seemed to mostly listen as he talked to our parents. All I see him do is nod and confirm questions.

"Yeah....yep...that's what happened Mom! No we're good...Okay love you too, Dad too. Oh and remember to call our cell phones and keep calling them...because we got rid of them already...yeah that's the point...everyone will think you didn't know...you know plausible deniability? Yeah and keep calling em' periodically. Yeah...yeah we're fine. Alright...love you too. Bye." He then hung up the phone, almost whispering his goodbye. He took a deep breath before speaking again, this time to me.

"Alright, we're good. Let's go." He said as he started walking again. This surprised me that he was so quick to move on.

"Go? Already? You sure?" I asked, walking up to keep pace with my little brother.

"Yeah. We told Mom and Dad, so now let's just...get ready to leave you know?"

"Are you sure you're okay 'Heem?" I questioned, he seemed to be acting strange, almost too quick to move on from what was an emotional moment for me and had to be the same or something similar for him. He shook his head in response.

"I'm good man. We just gotta move on and leave. Best to move forward before something happens." He replied. It sounded like good logic, but not typical Jaheem logic. Regardless, I let it go for now and continued walking with him. The two of us walked around the town a bit before deciding to talk and figure out our next steps.

"So what now?" Said Jaheem. "We just leave and head to the border?" It was a decent question, if not an obvious one.

"Yeah, pretty much. We need to get the supplies we need and get out as soon as possible." I explained.

"So...get back to the car then and just drive to Mexico?" Asked Jaheem, perplexed at the simplicity.

"Exactly. Let's go." I responded as I beckoned him to follow me back to the car. We retraced our steps, walking back towards the store from the payphone, past the hiding spot for the groceries, and back to the parking lot of the store. As we got closer, some caught my eye, causing me to place my hand on my brother's chest, stopping him from moving.

"Jaheem." Is all I said as I stared at what was probably my worst nightmare at the moment. There were several cop cars in the parking lot and several cops surrounding our car, searching and taking notes. They were looking for us, and we had nearly walked right into their hands and presented ourselves to them in a gift-wrapped package. Luckily we were a good 200 meters from them, so we were far enough away for them not to notice us.

"What?" Asked my little brother, agitated at me touching him like that.

"Look." I replied, pointing to the parking lot full of policemen. He squinted his eyes and leaned his head forward a bit, before they widened in shock and a bit of fear.

"Oh sh—" He started before I cut him off.

"Yeah, we got cops on our tail. Looks like driving's out since they've got the car bruh and there's no way they're letting it go. We'll have to walk to Mexico instead. It'll take longer, but at least it's safer." I explained. Jaheem nodded silently as he stared down the cops who were swarming the car and spread throughout the parking lot. He was focused and very intense.

"Yeah, let's go before they see us." He said in agreement as he began walking back the way we came.

"Of course." I said as I moved in the same direction. It was a silent walk as we cleared a few blocks, both of us deep in thought and contemplation. Finally after some time, 'Heem got impatient and spoke.

"So...restaurant's out of the picture. So is driving. Are we really going to walk to Mexico?" He pondered out loud, and somewhat at me as well. I could see why he would question it as it would take forever, but we had no real other choice.

"Yeah, that's our only option at the moment. The car is gone, and we don't have another way to travel besides our feet. So we have to make due." I explained.

"Alright, that makes sense, but since we can't go to a restaurant, how are we going to eat?" He questioned. It was a decent point. I wanted something substantial in my stomach before we started truly going on the run, once a news report got out. A restaurant was obviously not a possibility, but there had to be something similar...something more open with less wait time and cheaper prices. Then it hit me: a grocery store! No, not for like fruit or anything bagged or canned, but for an actual meal. Most grocery stores had some form of a restaurant or place to order, and I knew at least one that did, though it wasn't all that close. Though that wasn't an issue as it was best to get away from this general area anyways, given the cops that were crawling around. With that determined, I answered my little brother with certainty.

"Easy, 'Heem, the grocery store. They always got something you can order and I know one personally that has some good food." I described.

"A grocery store? Didn't we just leave 1—no, 2 of those?" He asked, a bit confused. He was right, but we weren't thinking about that then. I mean I'd like to be all-knowing, but sadly I wasn't quite there yet. So I

34

had to settle for thinking of things when they applied and when they were necessary.

"Yeah, but we didn't want to eat then. Now we do, so let's go. And before you ask, we're going to a different one, a few blocks down from that payphone we just used." I said, cutting off any questions he might've had. And so we walked...and walked...and walked...and walked. We walked block after block, past several groups of people, buildings, and other establishments. On the way we did talk a bit here and there about inconsequential things, mostly what we wanted to eat, the menu at the grocery store, and other banal topics. For example:

"Yo 'Bari, where exactly are we going? And what kind of food they got?" Questioned Jaheem.

"We're going to Jay's. And they got everything pretty much. Subs, barbecue, Chinese food, fried chicken, everything."

"Oh alright. Cool. What you getting?" He asked, keeping the conversation going.

"I don't know, probably a sub. It's definitely the most filling of the choices, even if it doesn't taste the best. And it's not like subs are nasty." I answered, thinking of the pros and cons of all the choices. Fried chicken and barbecue were pretty filling and good, but I just had both barbecue and chicken back at the restaurant, and despite how dumb it was (eating at the restaurant), the action wasn't erased from time or anything. It still happened. Thus I had the taste for something else.

"That's alright I guess. Me, I'm getting a bucket of fried chicken. It's the best tasting and filling enough to me. Unlike you, I didn't already have chicken." Responded Jaheem. That's right, he didn't have chicken, just a burger, so he wasn't suffering from the same chicken fatigue I was.

"Whatever man, if you want greasy fingers like that, be my guest. I won't save you if you can't escape because you can't grip a door handle." I said, teasing 'Heem about his choice as a big brother should. The thought of that being the reason for capture was funny enough to mask just how tragic it'd be in my mind. Like an old time black and white cartoon or something. It was funny enough that I had to stifle a chuckle.

"Yeah keep laughing, but when you're eating that stale bread and I'm eating that crispy goodness, we'll see who comes out on top." Was his quick response, biting back at me with a grin. The smiles didn't leave our faces for another block before they returned to normal. We walked another block when Jaheem touched my arm. I looked over and noticed an expression of concern on his face. He leaned in close as he spoke.

"Hey did you notice everyone staring at us as we walk? Seems like no matter where we go, people's heads turn. Like Inception or something." I did know what he meant. I had a similar experience, but quickly

35

chalked it up to my personal paranoia. I realized how implausible it was that *everyone* would be staring at us, even if they did know what we did. So clearly it wasn't really happening, it was just my (or our now) mind(s) playing tricks on me (us).

"They don't know if that's what you're asking 'Heem. And yes and no. I noticed them staring, but that's only because we feel a certain way and are looking for people to be staring at us. It's all mental." I explained. He seemed not to truly accept my explanation as he slowly nodded with a skeptical expression on his face.

"Alright, man whatever you say." He responded and was quiet until we got to Jay's, at least several more blocks of walking. It seemed to really shake him up. Finally after a long time of walking, we arrived at Jay's, ready to order our food. Slowly we walked in, heads on a swivel as we made our way to the side of the store, where the place to order food was. We got there with no real fanfare and separated to retrieve our food. Before we did however, I stopped Jaheem to make sure.

"Bruh, you alright?" I asked, placing my hand on his shoulder. He didn't even react much to it. He just nodded and spoke.

"Yeah, I'm good." He then walked forward and into the line for the fried chicken. It was a buffet type line where people filled their own containers, so it wasn't that crowded. Seeing he was good for now, I walked over to the sub line and waited as I was about 5th. It was a good 10 minute wait, as I kept my head on a swivel, making sure no one was tailing us or near us. I noticed that my brother had already filled his container and gotten the necessary sticker from the scale (these things usually cost per pound), and was waiting on me, impatience obvious in his eyes. I looked at him and shrugged as I had nothing. All I could do was wait. After another minute, I was finally up to order.

"Hello sir, what can I get you today?" Asked the clerk as I stepped up. He was a young Hispanic male with glasses.

"I'll take..." I trailed off as I forgot to pick what kind of sub I wanted. I didn't want to draw attention to myself however, so I quickly picked the first thing that came to mind. "I'll take a steak sub please, large. Lettuce, tomatoes, onions, pickles, and cheese please." I answered after the initial pause.

"OK, your sub will be ready in a moment. Thank You. Next!" Said the clerk. I stepped aside to wait for my sub and somewhat wondered how I could've been waiting for so long if my order took so little time. I did realize that others might not have been so decisive and likely asked questions or made up their minds on the spot (like I did, but with a lot more wait time). Shaking my head of these thoughts, I waited in place, foot tapping for my sub to be down. Jaheem kept pointing to his wrist, as if he had a watch and again I could only shrug. I wasn't in control here. I waited for only 2 minutes before my sub was finished. I quickly thanked the clerk, and took my bagged sub, as I followed my brother out of the area. We cut through the store, getting right to the entrance before getting in line to pay for our food.

"Damn, man what took so long?" Asked Jaheem. I merely rolled my eyes.

"You saw what took so long: everyone was ahead of me in line. And then they had to make my sub. I was only ordering for a good 10 seconds, not sure what you're talking about." I countered.

"True. But still, time is of the essence man. We don't got none to waste." He responded. I nodded in agreement. He was right, if we could, it'd be best to avoid anything like this again. No use waiting in the same area for a long time so cops could run up on us. Albeit it was much better than a restaurant where the wait time was close to an hour minimally, so there was some good in comparison.

Quickly we zig zagged through the store, as we cut to the front, where the cashiers were. The lines were pretty long and any onlooker could see the disappointment etched on our faces. My brother was the first to vocalize his.

"Man, how busy is this place? Every line is full though? We don't got time to waste like this. I'm not trying to..." He trailed off, not daring to put that last thought into existence. At least not in a public place and in broad day. I nodded in agreement as I scanned the lines, looking for an opening we could make it into, an express line, a less than 12 items line, anything where it'd be quick. A few moments later I spotted just that, an express lane with only 4 people in it, hidden deep within the crowd of shoppers, on the tail end of the various cashier lines, all the way to the left. I touched Jaheem's arm and gestured to the lane, pointing it out to him both physically and verbally.

"Yo look, there's one on the far end over there. Only 4 people and it's an express..." I too trailed off much like 'Heem did seconds ago. Not because I had a thought I didn't want to put into existence, but the opposite: I had a thought I *did* want to put into existence—scratch that a though I *needed* to put into existence.

"What? It's an express lane? Then let's go! Why'd you stop like that?" Questioned my little brother. I shook my head as I spoke in a low tone so others couldn't hear us.

"Never mind bro. We can't go in that lane. We don't got the funds, if you know what I mean. We got to skate out of here without being seen. That's the main issue." I said as I leaned in to his ear. His expression changed from one of confusion to one of understanding.

"Oh, right. Yeah. We'll be fine bruh. Just walk through and act like we should be able to walk through, guarantee nobody will try to stop us. By the time they catch us on cam or whatever, we'll be…in the Promise Land." He assured me. His words kind of made sense, as I didn't see any kind of sensors at the entrance of the store if I was honest. It seemed like they relied mostly on the cameras and fear of being caught. While those both applied to us, by the time they came to fruition, we'd be gone, so we really had nothing to fear. So with a deep breath, I begun walking and beckoned my brother to follow my lead. We simply walked around the cashiers, past the lotto playing and customer service booths, and were on our way out the door. That's when it happened. That's when, as we were leaving, I saw something on the TV over in the corner, near the lotto playing section where they always had the news going.

What I saw was a news report about an incident with some cops and some teens earlier in the day. My heart sunk and my eyes widened as I realized that was probably us. Just as it crossed my mind, did the proof cross the TV screen and our pictures were plastered on the screen, taken from our yearbook pictures. I nudged Jaheem and whispered to him.

"TV. 'Heem, the TV. They got us." His eyes snapped up and he turned quickly, seeing us on the screen. He cursed under his breath and immediately turned back around and jetted. He physically ran, seemingly at top speed out of the store. I was going to follow him, but I knew running would bring suspicion so I calmly turned around with a deep breath and fast-walked out of the store, desperate to get away from the situation and find my brother. I walked out of the doors and immediately spotted my brother waiting for me on the side of the window, not visible from inside store. I walk by him and motion for him to follow, as I take a few steps (an understatement as we nearly walked an entire block) and then turn into a random alley. He's there seconds after me and we both take a few deep breaths.

"So it's really happening." He said, sounding sad and disappointed at how things turned out. His head was down and he shook his head as he spoke. "I can't believe, it's really happening."

"Yeah, it's insane, but it's here now. We waited too long too. We need to leave the country ghost speed. And probably change how we look to keep off suspicion." I explained. Changing our looks would be a good move as the removal of even the tiniest features whether it'd be hair, facial hair, eye color, clothing style etc. could easily make a person unrecognizable. Even people close to the person might be fooled. 'Heem didn't seem to think so as he rolled his eyes when I said it.

"Well duh. We're on the run; of course we need to change how we look. That's fleeing 101, the basic, the breaks. We need to get to the barbershop yesterday and get our hair cut." I thought on his words for a while, weighing the pros and cons of it, but overall it was too risky. What if someone identified us at the barber shop? Then we'd just be shaving our heads for our eventual prison sentence, if we were that lucky. From what we experienced earlier, the cops would probably roll up and gun us down, no matter what we said. I make my thoughts known to my brother, voicing my disapproval.

"No, we can't go to the barber shop, not now. Our descriptions are out and will be very similar to how we look now. We can't go anywhere or be seen anywhere looking like this. We need new...everything: clothes, hair, shoes, everything." Jaheem didn't understand and looked taken aback at my suggestion, mad almost.

"That's what I'm *trying* to do with the barber!" He replied, raising his voice. I shook my head in response.

"I know, but it's too risky. If they see us, we're done. Whether it's the barbers themselves, people in the barbershop, people passing by the barbershop, if they see us, we can get caught and then our life is over." I described to him once more why this was a bad idea. He nodded at my explanation, but scared me by responding to the last part, mumbling the words under his breath.

"Not without a fight." I wanted to correct him, tell him not to talk like that, not to treat the cops as our enemy but...I really couldn't. They definitely were in this case and he might be right. Still, I didn't want us to feel like we had to fight as soon as we saw a cop and actually become the murderers they think we are. It took some time, but eventually I mustered up the courage to respond.

"Don't say that."

"Say what?"

"Not without a fight. Just let them arrest you or they might end up killing you." I pleaded, knowing it might not be an option, but if it was it was the option I wanted him to take, as he just gets more aggressive when confronted.

"Or I might end up killing them!" He yells back. I shook my head.

"Just don't man. I don't want my baby brother dying like that. It doesn't have to be like that." I said, trying to calm him down so he wouldn't do something reckless. Even though in the back of my mind...

"But it will be. We saw how they were when we did nothing wrong! They tried to arrest us and beat us down, shoot us even! Now that we're cop killers...I don't trust them pigs not to shoot on sight. So I'm shooting first." He replied with more aggression. The sad thing is that he wasn't necessarily wrong. The cops were acting crazy *before* me and 'Heem were designated cop killers. It was very likely they'd simply pull up and shoot on sight now that we were. But still, what did he mean by shoot first?

"Shooting first...? With what?" I shouted in confusion at the tough talk my little brother was spouting.

"This." Said Jaheem as he pulled out two guns. I recoiled at the sight of the guns, almost having flashbacks, and was appalled that 'Heem had somehow acquired guns in the short time we were on the run together.

"Where'd you get that!" I shouted in surprise and wonder. Where does a 14 year old get guns from anyways? Somehow Jaheem had returned to being completely level headed and acted like this was as normal as talking basketball.

"The cops. They're dead. They don't need 'em, we do." He answered nonchalantly, actually shrugging as he spoke. I shook my head frantically and somewhat in fear.

"We don't need those." I protested, not wanting to give anyone more ammo or a more of a reason to try to kill me.

"Yeah we do." He countered.

"No we don't. We're not having a shootout with the cops!" I exclaimed loudly, asserting my authority over my brother. He looked down and seemed to relent. Finally he held out one of the guns in my direction, handing it over.

"Fine. Just in case then." I stared at the gun for what was likely only 10 seconds, but felt like hours. Finally I reach my hand out slowly, shaking as I do and take the gun.

"...just in case." I muttered.

"I got a taser too." Added in my brother. I...I didn't care anymore so I remained silent for a good while, realizing just how dangerous the situation we were in was, that my little brother felt the need to retrieve guns and a taser. And the sad part is that he wasn't even wrong.

Chapter 4: Fleeing 101

After a minute of silence Jaheem was the first to speak, changing the subject back to what it was before he volunteered that he had guns: our hair.

"...So back to the hair, what do you want to do then, if not the barber?" He asked sincerely, confused on the next step. I thought about it for a moment and we didn't have many options. The only thing I could think of was to somehow disguise ourselves before entering the barbershop and then getting a cut that way. Maybe...yeah I suppose we could do that.

"I say we cut it ourselves." I put forth the answer in a calm voice. This was our only option. 'Heem didn't like it of course.

"What!?" He asked a bit loudly, shocked by my answer.

"Nah, I mean, we can still go to the barbers to get our hair looking right, just AFTER we cut it ourselves. So they don't notice who we are." I clarified. Jaheem's eyes changed to eyes of understanding as I did and he nodded in agreement before he asked his next question.

"So we stealing new clothes too then right?"

"NO! We're *buying* new clothes..." I trailed off, realizing we didn't have enough money left to do that. Sighing in resignation, I changed my answer. "OK yes we're stealing clothes. Stay simple though. A hat, something to cover our faces, and sunglasses. That's the first things we need." Once we had that, it'd be hard to tell who we are, and then we could change the rest of our clothes a lot easier.

"Alright then, I guess I should start taking my hair out?" Jaheem asks. I thought about it, and that'd be the easiest way for him to change appearances. It wasn't a huge difference, but someone who's unfamiliar with him would probably think he was a different person. I nod in affirmation. "Yeah that first. In fact, you don't have to do much but take your braids out before getting it cut. I'm the one that needs to do some self-grooming." I explained as I didn't have an easy fix like taking my hair out or anything like it. I just had an afro. I guess I could try patting it down to go out in public, but the barber would likely just pick it out before cutting it, putting me right back in the same circumstance as I am now.

"Oh alright then. I'm getting a high top fade. You?" Of course my brother wanted to discuss style in a serious situation like this. It didn't really matter to me, so I chose something basic.

"Probably a low cut just to look completely different. Also cutting off my facial hair." Jaheem caught what I was going for, whether he meant to or not.

"So you going to look like a whole different person then."

"Yeah, that's the objective." I confirmed. We wait in the alley for a few moments of complete silence and contemplation. Again Jaheem is the one to speak up.

"So how do we get into the store to buy stuff anyways? We look EXACTLY the same right now and there's nothing to cut our hair with here." He had a good point really. I thought of it but still didn't have much of a solution. All I could mutter is a quick phrase as I continued thinking.

"I'll think of something." It takes a few minutes as I think over what we have on us that can make us look totally different. I had shorts underneath my pants so that could help, and 'Heem had a du-rag for his hair...that's right! Jaheem's du-rag.

"'Heem let me use your du-rag." I said quickly, holding my hand out. Jaheem looked confused but nodded, shrugging as he handed it to me. I put it over my head, tying it as I do and pat down my hair as much as possible. I looked positively silly, but also different, which is good. After that, I took off my shirt and my pants, leaving me topless with basketball shorts, a du-rag, and my shoes on. I successfully have transformed into a totally different person. I can see the confusion on Jabari's face as he asked his question.

"Wait why don't you just look like that rather then get new clothes?" I shook my head before responding.

"Because I ain't trying to be half naked all the time." Was my response, a bit snippy but true. I had the ability to take my shirt off because of my athletic cut, but didn't exactly want to be in that state of dress 24/7. I then held out my hand and spoke. "Let me hold your money Jaheem. I'd rather buy the stuff we need than continue stealing."

'Heem rolled his eyes but handed me his money. I then walked out of the alley and down the street, searching for the nearest grocery store. It was about 3 blocks down when I finally saw one and entered through the door. My eyes scanned the store for what we needed, looking for shaving cream, a razor, some scissors, some paint, some glasses, and some sun glasses. It didn't take too long, though I ended up walking throughout nearly the entire store due to everything being in different aisles. After a good 5 minute trip, I had my cart ready with what I needed and brought it to the register. The line wasn't too long, only about 3 people and I wasn't too nervous as 'Heem was right, I looked like a totally different person. Finally I got to the front of the line and placed my items down on the belt. The cashier scanned them quickly and then spoke.

"That'll be $11.38 sir." Instinctively I reached for my credit card before remembering that it'd be tracked if I did. Coming to my senses, I dug in my pockets and retrieved our money, paying with a $5 and a $10. The cashier took my money, gave me my change and I quickly left the store after wishing him a good day.

"Have a good day."

"You too, thank you."

Another 3 block walk and I was back to our spot, handing the bag to Jaheem as I took out the razor and shaving cream. A good look at him told me that he spent the time taking out his cornrows, and he was about halfway through. Good, it wouldn't take long for me to shave so we might be done at the same time and ready to go. I put the cream on my hand and slathered it over my face, before using the razor to cut everything off. No facial hair to be seen. It only took a few minutes, so I took out the scissors and began on my hair. A few minutes of uneven cutting later, I had nothing left on my head but an irregular amount of hair roughly an inch from my scalp. I left it like that for the time being as the barber would clean up anything else. At this time, Jaheem spoke again as he worked on unraveling his cornrows, almost finished.

"They ain't have no shirts?" I shook my head. In truth I didn't exactly look for shirts, but grocery stores rarely had them. I was positive this one didn't have any clothing in it either.

"Nah, but I got what we needed and what I could. I did get us a pair of glasses and sunglasses to wear to help the disguise." I then reached into the back and pulled out the cheap, normal glasses and gave them to Jaheem. "Here put these on." I commanded as I took the sunglasses for myself and kept his du-rag. He listened as he put them on and ran his fingers through his hair, making sure it was all set for him to go out.

"Hurry up with that hair man. I need you to go out to the clothes store and pick us out something. And don't try to be stylish, just pick out the first passable thing in our size." I commanded as he continued working on his hair for a few minutes after he put on the glasses.

"Calm down, I'm working on it." Was his response. I shook my head, I wish he'd took this more serious. He continues working on his hair for an entire hour, claiming he had to look fresh, and that he had trouble unraveling the last few ones as 'they're always the hardest.' I almost had a panic attack in the meantime, looking around for cops, or witnesses, or anything or anyone that could get us caught. It was a nerve-wracking hour, and time wasted in my opinion, just to satisfy my brother's feelings of vanity. Finally after that hour, Jaheem shed his shirt and used his new glasses and new hair style to camouflage as he walks down the street only a block away, and into the clothing store.

I waited and waited and waited and waited for 'Heem to come out, but the longer I waited, the more worried I became. Maybe he ran into some cops in there and they had a shootout? No, I didn't hear any guns. Maybe he got into some kind of fight then? Or they had him tazed and were waiting, using him as bait to lure me out then? Or maybe something else happened to him and some shady guy stabbed him or something? Tons of scenarios went through my head until after thirty minutes of waiting, I went in with my same disguise, shedding the sunglasses as they'd be suspicious, and looked for my brother. I fretted for 5 minutes, looking all over the store for him, trying to get a glimpse of him anywhere until I got into the men's section. To my...disappointment, rage, annoyance, and frustration this fool was actually shopping leisurely, looking for the greatest fashion and passing over clothes! Was he an idiot?! Did he just not take this serious?! Did he understand how dangerous this whole thing was?! The thoughts passed through my mind as I walked up to confront him, hands shaking as I did.

"What are you doing!" I whispered harshly, grabbing him by the shoulder. I could see in his bag he had picked out a vest, a jacket, some sneakers, a hat, and some designer clothes. Jaheem jumps as I grab him, but calms down once he sees it's me.

"Calm down man, I just got done picking out my clothes. I'm good now, we can go." He spoke nonchalantly. I'm livid and it took all I had not to actually shout and bring attention to us.

"Picking out your clothes?! Jaheem we're on the run, we don't have time to pick out fashionable clothes and shit! You almost made me blow our cover because you're taking your time picking out clothes?!" I blew up at him, as I whispered harshly once more, my eyes held my disappointment and rage as they bore holes into him. I stared him down and he was silent as I shook my head and went shopping for myself. I looked quickly and picked out the first few things I saw that were my size, some t-shirts that were black, red, blue, and whatnot, some jeans, a jacket, and a hat. I was done in less than 5 minutes. I returned to Jaheem's spot and gave him a pointed look.

"See how quick that was? That's what you were supposed to do! For both of us!" I lectured, genuinely disappointed in Jaheem's nonchalant and absolutely stupid behavior. Jaheem remained silent for a moment longer as I collected myself and my thoughts. We still had to devise a way to get this out of the store and it wouldn't hurt to have 'Heem's input.

"So now," I began as I paused to think my words through carefully. Never knew who was watching or listening. "We have to figure out how to take these with us. We got to get the tags off somehow..." I reminded him, trailing off. He looked up slowly from his silence and seemed to think for a moment before presenting his answer.

"Yo, just carry the stuff and run." He said with a shrug. Wha...I...I was at a loss for words to be honest. My brother couldn't be this dumb, this simpleminded. He was a smart kid and I thought devious as well. Maybe he was just naïve to how things worked. It was my job to teach him after all. With a sharp inhale, I reply in a scalding tone.

"Dumbass that's how we get caught. We don't want to alert *anyone* to our presence. We get caught stealing, they call the police, and then...well it doesn't end good." He didn't seem too affected by my tone or disparaging comments. He did however respond with a frustratingly unhelpful question.

"Then how do we do this?" He asked. I gave him a look after that one. If I knew, we wouldn't be discussing this.

"I don't know..." I said, trailing off to think some more. There had to be a good and easy way to get these clothes out of the store without getting caught. I was distracted from my thoughts by Jaheem who seemed to think he had an idea.

"Yo I got it. I go and find the fire alarm, pull it, and while everyone is scrambling to get out, you jet with the clothes." He explained as if it was the most obvious plan in the world. I supposed that it would work despite how simple it was, so I nodded slowly in response.

"Okay, that's...a plan I guess. Just make sure to use your shirt or they'll get your fingerprints and know we were here. We don't want to leave them any clues or any way to trace us." I warned 'Heem before he wandered off to find said fire alarm.

"Yeah, okay." Was his response as he nodded and then walked off to find a fire alarm to pull. Meanwhile I inched closer to the exit so there'd be less distance to run and less suspicion as I'd be running for a far less time and distance. I did it naturally of course, continuing to look at clothes as if I needed them, sizing them up with me, staring at certain items as if I was thinking about them, the whole works. After a minute or so it finally came, the screeching sound of the fire alarm.

"Guess it's time." I muttered to myself as I stuffed our clothes into the bags from our other groceries, tied up the bags, and took off running. As a natural athlete I overtook the other customers who tried to run or move quickly, and easily beat them out of the store. The alarm sounded when I ran past, but everyone was more worried about a different, potentially more dangerous alarm. 'Heem was right, the plan worked and now we had our clothes. I kept going for a bit, getting away from the store in general, and ran over 20 meters before braking so 'Heem could catch me. After slowing down to a walk and walking for 5 minutes, I decided to simply head towards our little alley way and meet him there. If he hadn't caught up to me by now, he likely wasn't going to.

I was in disbelief when not a second after that thought, Jaheem was in sight, running up to me, but I shrugged it off as the whole 'speak of the devil' situation. I thought about him catching up, and so he did, though it almost worked in reverse since I doubted his ability to catch me, but all that ends well...

"Yo, I told you that'd work man! I told you!" Exclaimed Jaheem as he got within range, about 5 meters. I just shook my head and rolled my eyes.

"Yeah 'Heem, tell the whole world that it was us. That'll help out our situation *a lot*. Shout it to the heavens! Matter of fact, call the cops right now and just turn us in." I responded sarcastically. Now he actually did a good job of not mentioning what 'that' was that worked, but still...we were too close to the store to be shouting it so loudly in the streets. He waved me off however, not seeing the big deal as he reached me, stopping to walk by my side. While catching his breath a bit, he responds.

"Sure man. All I can say is 'called it'. I'm definitely the mastermind of the family, sorry 'Bari." He responded excitedly. He then held out his hand, waiting for me to slap him up while a big grin adorned his face. I just glanced at the hand and then at his face and kept on pace. He rolled his eyes at the rejection and walked with me to our spot in silence.

"So..." He began, as he now breathed normally. "We got the clothes, we got the hair, we got the disguises, so what's next?" He asked with curiosity lacing his voice. I thought about it for a moment. Ultimately we pretty much just wanted to leave. Go, travel until we get to Mexico and get off scot-free. For now, we just needed a place to sleep and to take care of some business, make sure the cops can't track us.

"I mean the next step is to just go to Mexico really." I explained. "But it's late so we just need to find somewhere to sleep...somehow and make sure we're not being tracked." Realization hits Jaheem as he nods in agreement.

"Ah, we got to get rid of our phones then."

"Yeah, then go sleep." I confirmed. He took out his phone as I did mine and we walked to a nearby garbage can. I made the motion to throw mines in, but noticed that my brother froze, so I too stopped. I wondered why he hesitated, and didn't want to make a mistake at this point.

"What?" I inquired, curiosity now lacing my voice.

"I get that we can't keep our phones 'cause of GPS and stuff, but how will we communicate if we separate? I know we discussed burner phones, but I actually don't know how to...you know, do that." He asked, uneasy about the whole process. I looked at him, perplexed that he'd be the one hesitant.

"Bruh, it was *your* suggestion, and a correct one. We can't keep these or they'll find us in a second. And then it's off to prison or the graveyard." He rolled his eyes a bit, clearly annoyed by what he saw as a condescending tone.

"Yeah I know that, I'm just worried that if we get split, we won't be able to find each other." He explained.

"I get it but...I mean the phones got to go. And it's nothing to be worried about. A burner phone's just a pre-paid phone and we can use something like...walkie-talkies until we get that." I offered.

"Walkie...where do we get walkie talkies?" A good question of sorts. I assumed that some store with electronics would do. So I said as much.

"I don't know man, some electronics store. We'll get it figured out, don't worry. Right now though? We need to get rid of these phones and that GPS tracking stuff." I pointed out. He shook his head as he dropped his phone in the garbage. I soon followed suit, taking mine out and dropping it in without hesitation. We both stared at the trash can for a while before he spoke up.

"So where are we sleeping again? Because staying near the trash can would defeat the purpose of throwing away the phones and...I'm not trying to sleep on the streets or in that alleyway." It was a decent point. We obviously couldn't sleep anywhere near here, and I personally also disliked the idea of sleeping in the streets. The longer I thought about it, we just needed any old building, a store that would close later would do. Make it a department store actually so we can pick up the walkie-talkies and the batteries and then bounce. It was the perfect plan. So naturally I shrugged in response.

"I don't know. I say we just...walk. Walk a few blocks from here and find some building that's about to close, best case a department store, to sleep in." Jaheem seemed confused by my statement and asked me to clarify.

"Why a department store? Like it doesn't sound bad, but why is that best case?" I smiled and pointed to my head.

"Because young Padawan, there we could get our walkie-talkies, batteries, and anything else we felt like getting. Hell if they have food, we could even swipe some snacks."

"Oooooh" Was his reply as he thought about the possibilities. "Yeah let's find that department store." And so we walked about 7 blocks, distancing ourselves from the phones as much as we could before fatigue started to take us. Then we started to look for a department store and walked past 3 non-department stores, 2 restaurants, 5 other unimportant buildings, and so on. Finally we located what we wanted and waltzed right in under the guise of shopping. As we entered the building, I whispered to my brother.

"Be on the lookout for cameras. Avoid them if possible and find a good spot where they don't exist so we can disappear and sleep. Meet up at the men's bathroom."

"Alright cool. I'll do that as I get the snacks. You can get the um...walkie-talkies or whatever." He replied as he walked in the direction of the food aisles. I was okay with that, so I started my trek towards the electronics section. I made sure to avoid as many cameras as possible, but once I needed to look for walkie-talkies, that became impossible. Still I found out and remembered various locations where we couldn't sleep so it worked out for us. Walkie-talkies weren't really in style so they didn't have much of a selection; even still I browsed a bit, looking between the three choices, trying to figure out which was best. There was one pair that had some red lining, looked like it had longer range, but shorter battery life. Another was all black and had pretty decent both, while the last pair had some grey in them and lasted forever with a shorter range. Ultimately, after 5 minutes of staring and comparison, I chose the first choice. I didn't anticipate being split up, but if we were, I didn't want something as stupid as range to separate us.

I picked the pair of walkie-talkies up off the shelf and began walking back to bathroom to meet Jaheem, when something caught my eye: the phones for sale. These could be our burner phones if we used them right, especially as we had no money. They wouldn't have any record of being stolen and thus no one could trace them to us. The more I thought about it the better sense it made...until I remembered that they would be reported stolen and once that happened the GPS would be tracked the same as if we had our own cell phones. So that plan was out. With a deep breath I walked by the phones and instead picked up something close to 10 packs of batteries, making sure they matched the type of the walkie-talkies, before heading back to the bathroom. When I got there, I saw Jaheem there with a bag of apples, some bananas, a jug of juice and a 24 pack of bottled water. Unfortunately he also had a box of cookies and a giant bag of gummy bears, seemingly foregoing health altogether with those choices. He looked happy and it wasn't too bad, but still I had to ask.

"Hey bro," I started off, acknowledging his presence. He looked up, expecting a question. "What's up with the cookies and gummy bears?" Jaheem just shrugged before answering.

"I don't know, we're on the run, life's not normal so I thought we could treat ourselves with some junk nah mean?" I nodded, getting his logic even if I didn't agree with it.

"Yeah but do we need all of that?" I asked, gesturing with my hands, referring to just how much he got. "Portion control is a thing, yo." He gave me a look before he replied.

"I get it, but this isn't the only place we're going to be. Might need some for later. So I got these." Well that got me nowhere, best to just let it go.

"Alright, then what about the cameras?" I asked, hoping he still managed to scout out the area for us. He looked ahead with a blank stare, spacing out as he tried to retrace his steps in his head. It took a few minutes, but it eventually came to him.

"Yeah, saw them out of the corner of my eye. Food aisles are off limits."

"Same with electronics."

"Damn. Makes sense though, those are the most expensive things in the store probably."

"Yeah, besides jewelry. Anyways, we need to split up, look around to find that spot so we can sleep. I'll get the men's clothes section, toys, and medicine, you get what's left. Sound like a plan?"

"Sounds like one to me." 'Heem agreed with a shrug and a nod.

"Cool. Let's split." I replied while sticking out my fist for a dab. Without fanfare, he met my fist and dabbed me up as we walked in opposite directions. First thing I checked was the men's clothes section. From what I could see, there's always at least 1 camera monitoring each area, whether it was shoes, kid's shirts, kid's pants, men's pants, men's shirts, shorts, jeans, underwear, hats etc. Every area was relatively locked down, even the changing rooms since they had cameras pointed directly outside of the entrance. Next I checked the medicine section as it was closer. There were only really 3 cameras in the entire section, watching the pharmacy area and spread out between the aisles. There might be a few spaces we can squeeze into individually, but that was far too dangerous given the situation, so I considered that a 'no' just like the men's clothes section. Finally I checked the toy section, boys and girls, and there were cameras on every aisle. So that too was a 'no.' I hoped that Jaheem had better luck. A bit downtrodden, I trekked back to the bathroom and waited for my little brother to do the same.

I waited for a few minutes before my brother returned looking triumphant.

"So what'd you find?" He asked nonchalantly as he walked towards me. I shook my head in disappointment.

"Nothing. All 3 were a bust. Cameras everywhere or the areas without cameras were too small. What you'd get?" I responded. His mouth widened into a smile as he replied.

"I got 2."

"2?" I questioned, in wonder of him finding multiple spots when I couldn't find one. And then to clarify…"Like 2 different sections without cameras?"

"Yeah, what else would I mean exactly?" He asked matter-of-factly. A good question really, but I was too shocked to understand at first so I ended up being rhetorical. It happens.

"I don't know man, just answer the question. No snark needed. Now what were they?" I inquired.

"The sections?" He clarified.

"No monkeys we saw when we walked in—of course I mean the sections 'Heem." I answered sarcastically.

"Oh alright. It was both the women's clothing section and the sports section." He said. We both stood in silence for a moment before giving each other a knowing look.

"Sports section it is then." I decided, knowing he'd agree with me.

"Yeah definitely." Was his retort. With that settled we walked over with our gear, found a good spot to sit in and just camped out. We munched a bit throughout the night, me eating an apple and a banana, drinking about a cup of juice and two bottled waters, and Jaheem eating a ton of gummy bears and cookies with some juice. We sat there, just chatting about life, not girls or basketball this time, but what we'll do after this situation.

"So in Mexico…" Jaheem spoke, trailing off. "Like what do we do?" He asked. A good question. We'd never been on our own before and now we' be doing it in a brand new country, what some call a lawless country.

"I don't know, start over I guess." I said, giving the obvious answer.

"Yeah I know but like…how? We've never worked or been on our own and now we're in Mexico with all those cartels, drug lords, and corrupt cops—even more corrupt than here, and any of them can end your life." He said, explaining his confusion. "Not that we'll let them end our lives, but still, it's going to be way tougher than here in U.S., almost impossible in comparison." He was right about...well everything. Us not working, Mexico being a more hostile environment, all of it.

"We'll have to either lay low and try to learn some basic skills: farming, gardening, cleaning, etcetera or just...embrace this life as criminals really. No other choice. Then once we get enough money, we move out of Mexico, across seas to another continent like Asia or Africa."

"Asia or Africa?" He questioned.

"Yeah, probably somewhere like China or Taiwan in Asia, or Nigeria or Ghana or something for Africa. Or hell, one of the other hundred countries there. Basically we just need to get out. " Jaheem just nodded at that. We both knew that it wasn't the greatest of plans, but it was a necessary one if we didn't want to live the rest of our lives behind bars. So we pretty much had to. Suddenly we heard a noise and stopped talking, moving, weary of what we just heard. Was it an employee checking on things before leaving? Or was it the police having found us, ready to take us away? It was nerve wracking to say the least. I looked over and saw Jaheem tensing up a lot; he was even more worried than me.

The sounds continued as the steps echoed throughout the aisles. As they get louder, I saw Jaheem put his hand on his gun, ready to draw it out. This shocked and appalled me. We weren't actually killers, and shouldn't be so ready to end someone's life. I expressed as much to my little brother.

"'Heem, put the gun down." I whispered to him, giving him a stern look. He ignored me and grabbed the gun tighter, partially drawing it out. I continued to shake my head and whisper to him. "No. No. Jaheem, put it *down*, we don't need this." He continued not to listen. Finally the steps got to us...and passed right by our area. It looked like the employee missed us, we were scot-free. I waited for the steps to get so light that they all but disappeared before speaking normally and scolding Jaheem for his unnecessary actions.

"What was that about?" I asked him, prodding for answers, for why he was so ready to kill. He answered me matter-of-factly like it was the most obvious thing ever.

"We'll die if someone sees us. The police are trying to kill us, we can't get caught. I'm trying to make sure we don't."

"No, we can't think that way. If we get caught I'll likely die in prison while you might be able to get out of Juvy, and live life. Don't do anything stupid to mess that up 'Heem!" I explain to him, raising my voice a bit at the end of my statement, actually snatching the gun from my brother's hands. If he wasn't going to act responsibly with it, he didn't need it at all. "I'm the one who killed the cop, and I'll confess if I have to. You're innocent in all of this." Jaheem shakes his head in disagreement.

"I'm an accomplice. A willing one." We then sat in silence for a long time, not knowing what to say to each other. I was touched by his willingness to support me, but wanted to get the message across to him that he didn't have to be so willing to sacrifice everything at the same time. Nothing came out though, so we just moved on and went to sleep, ready to face tomorrow.

We awoke early the next day, knowing we had to so we didn't get caught. Jaheem was the first to use the bathroom, and I warned him not to get caught.

"Don't get caught 'Heem. It's still early and the store is still closed, but there might be some employees here working." I pointed out to him.

"I got it man, don't worry." He replied, dismissing my worries as he walked off to the bathroom. I sat there, somehow simultaneously sleepy-eyed and alert, constantly swiveling my head and moving my eyes, while also being tired from recently waking up. I started to worry after about 10 minutes, but had to hold myself back and wait for 'Heem. He could just be using the bathroom for a long time and there was no reason to worry. Finally after 5 more minutes, he returned. Instantly I got up, now remembering my own need to use the bathroom, and walked swiftly to the closest bathroom. I quickly pushed through the door, found a stall, and emptied the contents of my bladder. I exited said stall, washed my hands, and made it back, before 7 minutes had passed.

"We heading out?" My brother asked as soon as I got back. I nodded and responded.

"Yeah." I said as I went over to pick up the bags and other supplies we bought and stole. Looking them over, I realized the purified water bottles seemed to be obsolete with the bottled spring water 'Heem took. Either way I figured we'd keep both since one was finite while the other should technically last forever. After we gathered our supplies, we headed for the entrance, eyes darting back and forth, on the lookout for any employees that decided to check in early. We got out without much fanfare and continued our trek to Mexico.

We spent the entire day walking in the direction of the border, passing by countless buildings, people, cars etc. After the first 6 hours, we sat down on a random bench to rest. The heat was unbearable as it usually is, and walking for that long had us both sweaty and hungry. I reached into the bag to eat yet another apple and a banana, while Jaheem did the same, but also added some cookies and gummy bears. I shook my head as it would only make walking tougher and likely mess with his stomach. After eating we continued to sit for a few moments, drinking water and just generally resting from the heat and physical activity.

"Woo! It's too hot to be doing all of this walking!" Exclaimed Jaheem. I agreed with him but we had no other choice.

"Yeah, it is, but we have to. Using my car would just make it too easy to find us and I don't know how to hotwire a car. Do you?" I replied honestly. Of course I'd love to take a car to Mexico, it'd be much, much faster. Jaheem seemed to think on it.

"Nah I don't either, but...like why don't we just take a bus or a taxi or something?" With that, he stumped me. That was a damn good question and I had no real good answer. I just didn't think of it. And now I felt like an idiot. After a smack to my head, and burying my head in my hands for a good minute I started to laugh.

"Hahahahahahaha!" The sounds exited my mouth as a bitter laugh escaped my throat. My brother just looked at me, bewildered.

"Yo, what's wrong? You ok man?" He asked, concerned for my well-being. I understood as I was laughing like a mad man, but it was so funny and stupid I couldn't help it. Still laughing all I could do was nod and hold up my hand as I let it out. I laughed for about a minute before calming down enough to talk.

"I'm good man, I'm good. It's just...there is none." I said, answering his question from before.

"There is none?" He questioned, perplexed at my answer.

"Yeah there is no good reason why we can't take the bus or a taxi. I just...didn't think about it." I replied, letting him know the source of my laughter. "And I feel so stupid, but at the same time it's just hilarious that it was so obvious really." 'Heem just stared at me with a blank face.

"Bruh..." He trailed off in disbelief. "You serious?" I simply nodded with a smile on my face, trying to hold back any further laughter. He sighed in annoyance before getting up. "Then let's go catch a bus or whatever. Anything's better than walking." He declared.

And so we walked back to normal civilization, on our way to the bus stop. On the way, we passed a mall and Jaheem signaled to me to stop and go inside. I gave him the stink eye for a moment, before questioning it.

"Wait, weren't we going to the bus stop? Why do you want to go to the mall all of a sudden? Whatever it is, getting to Mexico is infinitely more important."

"Chill Jabari, I'm just using the bathroom. After that we can sit down and get something to eat before we take the 20 hour bus ride to hell." He explained as if that was supposed to calm me down or make any kind

"Bruh, that's crazy dangerous. Who knows what kind of people or police are in there? And mall cops will definitely be on the lookout so they can make a big arrest and get their big break. We're better off just waiting until the bus ride is done." He looked at me with an exasperated expression on his voice.

"I'm *not* waiting 20 hours to use the bathroom. And I want some real food in my stomach man, not just fruit and candy. Now come on already." He said as he walked in the direction of the mall. I sighed a nervous sigh and followed him in. As soon as we entered, I felt like all eyes were on us, even if that was blatantly false. I couldn't help but feel that something bad was bound to happen if we stayed here too long. We walked straight for a while and then turned left, arriving at the food court.

"Just wait here for a second, and I'll be right out." My brother commanded as he left. I could only shake my head at how ridiculous he was being. This was definitely NOT worth the risk, by any measurement of any kind. Luckily we were in the far off corner, away from basically all human interaction, but that luck didn't last too long. I waited for about 2 minutes when a hand touched my shoulder. I jumped and turned around suddenly. As I did, my heart dropped before beating so fast that lightning would struggle to keep pace. It was a police officer and he looked like he meant business.

Chapter 5: Escape to Mexico

"Hey son, no need to be startled, I'm just going to ask a few questions to make sure you're not the guy we're looking for. We heard about some suspicious fellas in a grocery store not too far from here, and want to make sure. So answer these and then you can go home or carry on with whatever you were doing." He stated in a stern voice. I nodded meekly, more nervous and afraid than I'd ever been in my entire life. What if I stumbled? Or stuttered? What if he figured out who I was? Would I have to kill him? Would he kill me? Should I surrender? No I can't, what would happen to Jaheem? These questions all passed through my mind as I slowly and softly spoke.

"Yeah."

"Good." He said, taking his hand off of my shoulder and onto his waist. "OK son, first, what's your name?"

"Barry" I said as a reflex. I usually said 'Bari as short for Jabari, so it was the easiest and quickest name I could think of.

"Last name?" He asked, eye raised.

"James." I replied. Again it was close to the "J" "A" part of my name, so it was more natural.

"OK, Barry, and where you were yesterday morning?" Yesterday morning? He means when we had the run in with the cops. Of course. I had to think of something quick so I said...

"Hooping. Playing basketball." He didn't look like he bought it.

"Where? A park, your home, school? We need someone to verify your location. Provide an alibi Barry, I'm sure you understand." He responded. I gulped in fear and nodded once more before racing through my thoughts for answers. No one could account for me being anywhere because...I wasn't there. Maybe my Mom and Dad...

"Home." I answered quickly.

"Home huh? I see...And what are you doing here now?" This one was easy. The truth sufficed.

"Getting something to eat." I replied.

"Uhuh. And are you alone?" I stopped myself mid nod. No one goes to the mall alone to eat unless they're on the run like we were. No it's best to say I'm with friends.

"Nah, I'm here with a friend."

"Hmm...it checks out, but I need to take you in to the station just to make sure. You understand, we don't play with cop killers." He spoke as he reached for his handcuffs.

"Cop killers?" I questioned, feigning ignorance. He just grimaced at the question as he got his handcuffs out.

"Don't play dumb boy. Now just come quietly and we don't have to—" He's interrupted by a sort of buzzing sound. My eyes opened wide as I saw my little brother Jaheem tazing a police man in the back of the head. The cop fell, and Jaheem kept going at it. Tazing him several more times just to be sure. He then tucked the taser back into his pocket and took off running, screaming 2 words to me as he does.

"Let's go!" He yelled, as he hightailed it out of there. I took a breath and quickly followed him. Being the older and fast brother, I caught up to him rather quickly and overtook him before slowing down to keep pace. We swiftly ran out of the mall and down the street a bit before stopping to catch our breath. I didn't waste time in berating him once we stopped.

"What the hell was that?" I shouted in confusion.

"They were about to take you to jail, and I'm NOT going to let that happen. If I have to take down a few more cops, then so be it." He answered defiantly and with conviction. No, this was not what we wanted; we did NOT want to go to war with the cops.

"Again, we are NOT fighting the cops and NOT having a shootout." I said sternly.

"Yeah you made sure of that." Muttered Jaheem before raising his voice to talk normally. "We *should* have shot that employee at the store, he must've ratted us out to the cops."

"You're right, he probably did, but death is not the answer." I responded, acknowledging that his thoughts had merit, but not the killing part.

"Yeah, well I disagree entirely. It's kill or be captured, and I'd definitely rather kill." Replied Jaheem, meaning every word he said. And that scared me. That was a mindset that could escalate the situation far above what it needed to be. I felt like I was losing 'Heem to this messed up situation and there was nothing I could do to stop it. I let the silence ride before changing the subject completely.

"You wanted to get something to eat right? Let's do that, we can discuss this later." I said, surprising him (I could tell by the look on his face) and avoiding the dark scenario we were discussing. His eyes lit up as he agreed.

"Yeah, let's find a restaurant or something. I'm starving." He replied much more calmly than he was speaking before. "I mean, not a restaurant, but another grocery store or something maybe." He corrected himself, remembering how we agreed that a restaurant was an astronomically stupid idea. We walked a couple blocks before stopping at a random grocery store spot. I hesitated as we stared at the entrance, something in my body telling us not to enter. It was fine before, but now? We were on the news and people might recognize us. I didn't like it. I'd rather go somewhere smaller, that still had something to eat. Some place like…a gas station. Yeah that was it. I turned to my brother to express my feelings.

"Yo 'Heem, we can get something to eat, but not here." I said. He raised an eyebrow in defiance.

"Um…OK, why not?" He asked simply, not dressing up his words in the slightest.

"I…I just have a bad feeling about this place. Like if we walk in, we're done for." I explained, describing my gut feeling to him.

"OK, but what makes this different? I mean Jay's was fine, but this random grocery store isn't?" 'Heem questioned further.

"Well it's a myriad of things. One, I knew Jay's and right where to go to find the food. Here, there's a possibility that we'll be wandering around the entire store looking for the same thing, and there's no guarantee they have something similar. Two, we've been on the news now. With that many people in there, someone might recognize us and call the cops. I'd rather not take that chance. Add on that we're already 2 black males and thus automatically generate suspicion from a certain group of people? I'd rather not take that chance." I reasoned with him, in a long winded explanation. 'Heem looked down, contemplating my words as he did.

"Alright, so then what's the alternative? What's a smaller place where we can get food without being caught?" He asked genuinely, looking to me for the answer. Luckily I already had it.

"Gas station." I said simply.

"Gas station?"

"Yeah, we can find one off on its own, not near much else, and there should be like 5 people max in the store. They should still have hot stuff ready to order and eat, and while it's not the same quality, it's good enough for what we need." I said, justifying my choice.

"A gas station though? I guess. I'm not really trying to eat no gas station food, but...it does seem like the best choice we got. So let's go." He relented. And so we left, walking through town, trying to find a stray gas station to eat at. We passed several in the middle of town, but they weren't right for what we needed. Jaheem pointed them out to me (as if I didn't see them on my own), but we needed something more isolated. Several blocks later we still hadn't gotten far enough to my liking, but I could tell Jaheem was tired in more ways than one. He was slightly physically tired, but mostly was mentally tired, agitated, and needed to stop soon. So we walked another block before I turned to him to reassure him.

"Don't worry 'Heem, we don't got far to go. I guarantee you that we'll find what we're looking for in the next 3 gas stations we see." Jaheem looked at me skeptically.

"And if we don't? Then what? We just walk around town on a wild goose chase?" He asked, voiced laced with irritation.

"Nah. We'll stop at the 3rd one no matter what. I promise you." Was my response. Not the smartest plan, but by now we had to have reached a place not close to the rest of town. At worst, it'd be slightly more populated than we wanted it to be, and we could make do with that. Either way it'd be 100 times better than a grocery store and a million times better than a restaurant. Time seemed to slow down for me in anticipation as we continued walking. The 1st gas station came up quickly, but was far too surrounded by other buildings. There was an ice cream store, and a tire store surrounding it as well as a small motel across the street. Jaheem looked at me, as if asking 'is this good enough?' and I shook my head and spoke but a small sentence that said everything.

"Too many stores." It was simple and to the point and made one thing clear: we still had a ways to go.

The next gas station was a pretty long walk, serving only to exhaust us physically and mentally as we trekked along. This one was pretty good as it was very isolated, with nothing surrounding it, just as I wanted. The problem was that it appeared to be very popular due to its low prices. There were several cars in the lot, and a few more would turn in as the ones that were already present would leave. This constant flow of traffic didn't sit well with me, so when 'Heem glanced at me to see my reaction, I shook my head once more.

"Too popular." Were my words as we kept pace. The 3rd and final gas station was...alright at best. It was a little ways off, but nowhere near the distance that the 2nd was to the 1st. It had only 1 building next to it: the tire shop, and about 3 cars in the lot and they didn't seem to be self-replenishing like at the 2nd spot. It wasn't the total isolation I wanted, but it'd have to be the one we stopped at. I did make a promise to my brother

58

after all. Jaheem looked at me with an expectant look in his eye and all I could to is shrug.

"I guess. It *is* the 3rd one." I said, referencing my earlier promise. Besides, it wasn't *so* bad. Still relatively isolated with few people. At worst, what? 3 people would be inside and see us? We could handle that. Like I said before, it's much better than the alternatives in a restaurant and grocery store.

As promised, we made our way to the 3rd gas station, stopping to cross the street as we did. Traffic wasn't too heavy, so we just had to wait for 2 cars to pass before jogging across the street to the other side. Not even short of breath, we then walked in to the gas station, as I held the door for my brother to let him in.

The gas station was very...green in theme. Green-lined walls, green-lined counters, green shelves, etc. It didn't bother me really, it was just...green. Very noticeable. I could feel Jaheem staring as well and had to tap his shoulder to get his attention.

"Look around for any hot food or any menu of some sort." I told him. 'Let me know what you find' was the unspoken part, but that was obvious. He went left and I went right as we quickly searched the gas station store. I saw a bunch of snacks: chips, cookies, beef jerky, cakes, etc. before I came upon the hot food. Unfortunately the hot food was in the same vein as it was also sweets. Inside the little oven were donuts, bear claws, small apple pies, churros, cookies, and other pastries. Nothing we could use though. I walked back to the center of the store, shaking my head as I made eye contact with 'Heem who also appeared to be done searching.

"Nothing." I informed him. "Just snacks and pastries."

"Yeah same here basically." He responded. "Just small hot pocket type stuff. Nothing substantial." Damn...so now what? There was only one option left.

"We could always see if they have some kind of pizza up front at the counter." I pointed out.

"Yeah, but how are we going to get it? We can't exactly pay for anything." My brother countered in a whisper. He had a decent point. We'd basically be at her mercy and hope she'd give us the pizza before we paid so that we could take it and run. I expressed as much to my brother.

"I don't know, we have to hope she gives us the food before she asks for money and then just bounce." said with a shrug. My brother shook his head in disagreement, but went along with the plan nonetheless. Following the plan, we both walked up to the clerk, a middle-aged white woman, eyeing the menu behind her that was partially blocked by the TV behind him. The news seemed to be playing, but we didn't pay it much mind as we had a mission to complete. This was definitely the last resort. I didn't like looking people in the eye

59

like this, as they might recognize us if they've seen the news. That is why I left this as a last option and *only* as a last option. But still, it was necessary, so I stepped forward and spoke.

"Hey, you guys have pizza?" I asked simply. The woman smiled warmly before answering with a bubbly voice.

"We sure do honey. We got a deal, 2 slices for just 2 dollars!" She said excitedly. I didn't let my face betray my façade, keeping my expression normal. This was good, we had enough money to pay for that and could avoid what basically would've been a robbery. I wasn't up for committing many more crimes, even if it was to escape. I mean, I'd do it if necessary, but I really didn't want to. I looked back at Jaheem and shook my head, telling him the plan was off. His face took an expression that said 'really?' but I didn't care, my mind was made up. Turning back to the clerk, I answered with a straight voice that didn't express my excitement.

"Cool, we'll take 2 slices then." I said as I pulled out my money, ready to pay. The clerk smiled even wider somehow, something I didn't think was possible.

"OK, honey, 2 slices coming right up." She said as she went to the oven they had the pizza in and retrieved our slices. She put them on the counter, each in their own box, and I handed her the money.

"Thank you." I said as I took the slices and handed on to Jaheem as we made our way out.

"Have a nice day, honey." She said as we turned to walk out. Jaheem gave me the same look, this time speaking his thoughts, though very low.

"Really, 'Bari?" He questioned, as I had abandoned the plan completely.

"Really what?" I countered, pretending not to know what he was talking about.

"What happened to the plan?" He interrogated. I merely shrugged and expressed my exact feelings on the situation.

"Wasn't necessary." I said simply.

"Wasn't necessary?" He said with a raised brow.

"Yeah, no reason to cause conflict if it isn't needed. Especially in our situation." I explained.

"Hmm..." He said, thinking it over. It seemed to make sense to him, but he didn't want to admit it. I shook my head with a smile as Jaheem walked out of the gas station store, silent, and I began following him out.

Before I could leave, something on the TV caught my eye. My worst nightmare was up on the screen as the newscaster talked about...who else but me and my brother, and in our updated appearances.

"...Police say to watch out for these 2: Jabari and Jaheem Wilson, youths with a penchant for violence and murder. These 2 boys were previously known for violently killing 2 cops in a routine traffic stop and fleeing the scene. Now they've changed their looks, and have attacked yet another policeman, tazing him multiple times until he was unconscious. The word is to NOT engage these 2, but call 911 if you see them. Their appearances have changed however and now the oldest: Jabari has low cut hair, and the youngest of the brothers: Jaheem has what they call a 'high top'. These boys are dangerous and are a menace to society. Stay away and call the police." The newscaster said in a serious tone. She was an older woman with shoulder length blonde hair, and dressed in a dress-suit. As she spoke, sketches of me and Jaheem in our current clothes and hair was shown on the screen. They clearly used our old pictures and changed the features to be more grim and intimidating while our hair was drawn to match what we currently had. The lady kept talking as they showed hazy footage of us in the store hiding out and in the mall with the cop. This was...this was bad.

"Now let us cut over to the young man who saw the 2 brothers hiding out in the store where he works. The young man faced down the 2 gun-toting fiends and was able to contact police to drive them off." The lady spoke, spouting lies to the screen as it cut over to the employee from the store, a skinny brown-haired kid with pale skin and a long nose.

"So I stayed a bit late to make sure everything was okay so that I could close up shop. I walked down the aisles, when I saw the Wilson brothers, poised and ready to pounce. They had their guns drawn and pointed at me, but the older brother told...he told the younger one to 'kill me with his bare hands'. I was lucky that I knew the place better than they did, and I was able to hide in the employee closet and call the police. From there I just waited until help came. I was lucky to escape with my life." He testified with genuine emotion. What was this guy talking about? None of this even got close to happening. Why would he lie like that? Was he getting paid? Did the police put him up to this? To just lie so blatantly was just so...foreign to me. I couldn't understand it.

By the time that was over, Jaheem was next to me, also staring at the screen, or more like glaring at it. Remembering that our appearances had been described both visually and verbally, I wordlessly pulled Jaheem with me through the exit of the small store. I was sure the clerk was frightened by now and was on her way of calling the police, and we needed to get out of there.

"That was…" I started, not able to find the words.

"That was a bunch of bull. He lied! They lied! Blatantly too! That…that's just…" Exclaimed Jaheem, trailing off as he too looked for the correct words or word to end his statement.

"Despicable." I breathed out quietly.

"Yeah despicable. I mean, why lie? Why make us seem so much worse than we are? Why—"

"Because they need us to look like bad guys so more people are willing to help them. It's that simple." I cut him off, letting him know what I just figured out in my mind. "But we got to move on from this. Just go right to the bus station and hop on the ride to Mexico. We'll be alright once we get there." I reassured him. He nodded in agreement as we started walking in that direction with our heads low. We passed by countless people, buildings, and establishments as we made our way to the bus stop, hiding our identities the entire way. Finally a few blocks away, we arrived at the most well-known bus terminal, ready for the bus to salvation. I was somewhat surprised as I half-expected the police to have major bus stations staked out. They had to know that we were going to try to leave the country, and a bus was one of the few options we really had now that they'd taken our car. Maybe they were staking out the border with extra security or something? I hoped not as that'd make it awfully difficult to escape. I shook the thoughts from my mind to address my brother. No use thinking about it now as it wasn't too important at the moment. We had to get to the border regardless.

"Jaheem, sit down for now. I got to see how much tickets cost and what we need." I let my brother know. He hesitated, but eventually nodded and sat down on the bench, patiently waiting. I walked a few feet, looking up at the signs trying to figure out where to go for tickets to Mexico. After looking for a while I saw what I needed and made my way over. To my disappointment, there was an incredibly long line that couldn't have had less than 20 people in it. It was going to be a while before I got my answer. Sighing, I went to the back of the line and patiently waited. Slowly the line moved, my feet trudging forward about an inch every few minutes as people completed their orders. Complete boredom was the feeling as my mind rotted away from waiting for so long. After 20 minutes of waiting my mind began wandering, thinking of random ideas as well as our future in Mexico and wherever we decided to live permanently.

I imagined myself as some huge international basketball star, leading my team to victory and my country to a gold medal. I'd be the best point guard the country's ever seen, averaging 35 points per game, 20 assists, and 12 rebounds. Not to mention 7 steals and 5 blocks. I thought about my brother joining me on the team as we became the most fearsome back court in the history of the game. He'd likely average something like 40 points a game with his focus on his jumpshot. He wouldn't be quite as good as me, but he'd easily be second best in the country. I'd expand my stardom into establishing a football team in said country, American Football, not that soccer stuff, and then I'd be a star quarterback and the best player to play that too. I'd be like the Hank Aaron or Wilt Chamberlain of the game, establishing all of the records and holding them for years to come, if not forever. I couldn't help but to smile as I thought of my awesome future, what I could be, what I would accomplish. Not only that but what WE could accomplish, me and my brother side by side. We just had to get past this ugly situation, change our names maybe, or get some kind of diplomatic immunity. Actually thinking on it, if we didn't do something like that, there's no way we could ever be sports stars. With a frown on my face I realized that if we were that good we'd be recognized and likely extradited back to America where we'd stand trial. Maybe if we made them enough money, the country would protect us? I...I couldn't be sure anymore. Who wants war with the US over some basketball star? But then...would the US wage war over something so petty? My thoughts began turning dark and I didn't like it one bit, but luckily I was knocked out of my stupor when I heard a voice talking to me. I was next in line.

"Hello Sir, how can I help you?" Asked the woman behind the desk. She was an old black woman who didn't seem too happy to see me.

"H-hello. I was wondering um...how much for a ticket to Mexico?" I inquired, trying to keep a straight and confident voice.

"To Mexico? Like Mexico City?" She asked, raising an eyebrow. Of course, I forgot to think of a city we wanted to go to. We couldn't just say 'Mexico' as a blanket term, it was an entire country. Flustered and without an answer, I simply agreed with her.

"Yeah, Mexico City. How much?" I questioned.

"$250." Was her answer. My eyes almost bugged out of my head. $250? Seriously? That...we didn't have anywhere near that much money. We'd probably have to go rob someone or something just to even try to get that kind of money, and I didn't like the thought of extending my criminal record and making those people on the news inevitably 'right' about me and Jaheem. We weren't violent and we weren't criminals, but this situation might force us to be. Getting back to the situation at hand, I swallowed my surprise and went to talk, but she beat me to it.

"That, and you'll need a passport naturally." She informed me, eyeing me up and down as if she suspected something. Damn, that was out of the question. I had one, but I don't think Jaheem did. Even if he did, we didn't carry our passports around with us, so we wouldn't have access to them anyways. I know I don't.

"Thank you ma'am." Is all I could muster as I nodded and walked back to my little brother. When I got there he was half asleep on the bench with his hat down over his face. I even heard snoring. He did have the decency to try to look alert, but it looks like sleep won out with him. Shaking my head I put my hand on his shoulder and shook him awake.

"Wha-huh? Damn what took so long? You got our tickets?" He interrogated me immediately. I shook my head.

"Long line. And nah, we need $250 and passports. We got to find a less well-known bus company that will let us through. Once we get to the border itself...I don't know, but at least it'll take us there.

"$250? That's insane. How're we going to get that kind of money?" He rightfully questioned. All I could do was be honest with him.

"I have no idea outside of robbing some random store. I'd rather not but..." I trailed off. He nodded, understanding what I meant. If we had to do it, we had to do it.

"Yeah...I guess we got to go search for that other bus company then right?" He inquired. I guess he was right, we had no other choice.

"Pretty much. We have no other options so...let's go." I responded, beckoning him to walk out with me. We kept walking, head down and silent, for a few more blocks until we saw another bus terminal, this one for a company we didn't know. Perfect, they're less likely to ask us for a passport. I mean we'd need one for the border, but we'd cross that line when we got to it.

"Alright, you know the drill. Wait here and I'll see what we're working with." I commanded 'Heem.

"Yeah whatever. Wake me up when you're done." Was his response. This time it was much easier to find what I needed, and even better, the line only had about 5 people in it. Within 5 minutes I was up and asking my questions.

"Hello sir, how may I help you?" I was asked again by the person manning the line. This time it was a Hispanic man with a mustache and short black hair. He seemed a lot more friendly than the lady from before.

"Hello, I wanted to know how much for 2 tickets to Mexico City." I replied.

"Oh, Mexico City? That'd be about $110 per ticket, so a total of $220." He answered.

"Okay, and that's it?" I asked, subtly asking about passports and extra jazz.

"Yeah that's it. Departure is at 7:45 PM for today or 8:15 PM for tomorrow. I can give you more departure times for other days if you want, sir." I waved him off.

"No, no, that's good. We'll take tickets for 8:15 PM tomorrow, I'll be back then to buy them. Thank You." I said as I dipped out to find Jaheem sitting on the bench, looking surprised to see me.

"Didn't have enough time to go to sleep this time did you?" I taunted him.

"Nah, I guess not. We good?" He responded.

"Yeah, kinda. It's $220 here, but if we can get the money, we're fine. No passports needed...at least not to the bus company. I assume we'll be stopped at the border for stuff still."

"Alright, cool. Let's get that money then." He said, feeling a bit more jovial as we walked out of the terminal.

"OK, so we have to find a way to get the money before 8:15 tomorrow night, because that's the tickets we're going for." I informed 'Heem. He did a double take when I said that before screwing up his face.

"8:15 tomorrow? Wait, are there tickets for today?" He asked in disbelief. I sighed before I answered.

"Yeah, for 7:45 today."

"7:45? What time is it? 4?" He responded in a bewildered voice. I thought back to when I was in the bus terminal. I remember it being 4:23 PM, so I relayed the information to him.

"4:23. Why?" I asked, legitimately confused at the moment. He sucked his teeth giving me another look saying 'are you serious?' before he replied.

"Yo just give me the money we got now. I'll hit you up on the walkie-talkie or whatever when it's time. 'Ll get us the money." My hand reached into my pocket slowly as I hesitated to hand my money over. I didn't know exactly what Jaheem was going to do and didn't want him to do something risky. After fishing out my money, I held it in my hand away from my brother as I questioned him.

"I got the money, but what're you thinking? What're you going to do?" I could think of several things, robbing someone whether it was a store or just people, hustling people in basketball or racing or something, and playing dice or gambling in some way. Only the last 2 needed money to start, so it was likely one of those, and both could be risky as we were wanted. Rather than responding he just rolled his eyes and demanded the money once more with his hand. When I refused to give it, he sucked his teeth and screwed up his face again.

"Come on man, you don't trust me? Your own brother? Don't do me like that 'Bari. I got this." He said with such confidence that he actually convinced me to give the money over. But still I wanted to be safe so I had to ask.

"OK 'Heem, but you're not doing anything risky right? No one's getting hurt? No criminal activity?" He shook his head.

"Nah, man it'll be clean." He replied. I gave him the side eye as I finally gave in and put my money in his hand.

"Alright 'Heem. If you were doing that, you know you could count on me right? I'd want to be involved to protect you, make sure nothing happens to you." I informed him. He nodded as he took the money and counted it with a look of glee on his face.

"Yeah, I know bruh. I don't need no protection though, just trust me. Stand back and let me handle this. We'll be on the bus tonight. Guaranteed." He said as he pocketed the money and jogged off to do who-knows-what.

I watched him leave and instantly got nervous even as I went to sit down back at the bus terminal. Dark thoughts and fears creeped up in my head as I thought about what could possibly happen to my brother while he's out there trying to get us that money. What if he got robbed instead? Or beat up? Or shot even? I couldn't handle losing my baby brother like that, so my thoughts quickly traveled away from that and more to what he could be doing. I wouldn't put it past Jaheem to be robbing people with his taser, knocking them out and taking their money until it accumulated to the $220 we needed. I could also see him doing the same to some random store, tasing some poor random clerk in the process. I couldn't see him doing this before, but since we've been on the run, it seemed like he'd changed. It made me wonder about the other criminals I'd seen or heard about. Were they too just doing crime out of necessity? Much like us? We were in a completely different situation, but necessity was still the father of ingenuity, and in this case, the ingenuity could be crime. Desperation does a lot to a man or a woman, and me and Jaheem were proof of that. Never would we have thought to steal clothes or water bottles or food before this whole situation. Same with tazing a cop or skipping out on the bill at a restaurant. It really put everything in perspective when I thought about it, and that was scary. I was sympathizing with criminals. I really had changed.

I moved my thoughts back to Jaheem as I imagined him simply betting on 1 on 1 games or even 5 on 5 games, as he put it down on the court, taking on all comers. He was quick with good handles, much like myself, though he was more focused on his jumpshot which was water. So he had a good chance if he used this method, and I hoped it was the method he was using. My thoughts continued to wander for another hour before I heard some commotion on my walkie-talkie.

"Jabari! Jabari!" I heard as I fumbled for it and finally held it up to my face.

"Yeah I'm here. You got it?" I questioned, genuinely curious.

"Yeah I got it man! Let's go!" Was his response.

"To the Promise Land." I said as we ended communication. I stood up, cracking my neck and stretching my body a bit, as I waited for my brother to return. It only took a few minutes, less than 10, for him to walk in with a Cheshire grin that threatened to tear his mouth open. As soon as he saw me, he headed over with a hop in his step, clearly joyous at his triumph.

"Yeah, what'd I tell you man! Got that money easy!" He exclaimed as he we slapped each other up and ended with a hug.

"You told me man, I can't deny that. And from the looks of it, you put in work."

"Damn straight man. Now let's go get those tickets!" He replied. I nodded and motioned for him to walk behind me as I went back to the line from before. There were still only about 8 people in line, so the wait wouldn't be too much. It seemed like eternity for us though as we were all-but shivering in excitement. Finally we got to the front and were ready to get our tickets.

"Hello, how may I help you?" Asked the person behind the counter, this time an elderly white male.

"I'd like 2 tickets to the Mexico City bus for tonight please." I responded after inhaling and exhaling a few times to calm myself down.

"OK, that'll be $220." Said the elderly man. Smiling, I turned to Jaheem, holding out my hand, and he slapped it down with confidence. Quickly I counted it and saw that we had more than enough. I separated what we needed and handed it to the man.

"Thank you." He replied as he took the money and counted it as well. He seemed to determine that it was enough as he put it in his register and handed me the 2 tickets. "Enjoy your trip." He said as I smiled and nodded and took the tickets from his hand. Giddy with excitement, we left the line and waited eagerly for the bus to arrive. It was a 2 hour wait, but time flew by as we couldn't wait to get on that bus. We both knew that we had won. We made it. Everything was fine and the chase was over.

Chapter 6: Run

Finally the bus arrived and we were quick to run up to the vehicle, present our tickets, and take our seats in the middle of the bus as we sat together.

"Yo, we made it man. We actually made it." Said Jaheem quietly. "It's over." I couldn't disagree with him either.

"Yeah, we did it." That was all that needed to be said as words couldn't quite capture the bliss, couldn't capture just how happy we were to be done with fleeing like criminals. We waited for the bus to start as it was still gathering passengers. During the wait we began to talk about what could've been.

"Yo 'Bari, you ever think about what could've been? What would've been if this whole thing hadn't happened?"

"Yeah, a few times." I answered shortly. He looked at me as if he wanted me to keep going so I did. "I thought about it...and it'd be great. I'd continue starring in basketball and football, getting a scholarship in both, definitely a full ride, probably to Texas University. I'd be valedictorian in high school or something close, maybe salutatorian, at least top 5. In college I'd be a star in both, setting records, and becoming the first man to get drafted to both the NFL and the NBA, 1st round 1st pick too." I said, speaking my dreams more than what would actually happen. I knew that would actually happen would be close, I'd be in the top percentile in high school as far as grades go, and likely would get the scholarship. After that, I'd have to choose between basketball and football, and would likely choose basketball. Then I'd get drafted somewhere in the top 10 likely and have a good career. Oh right, I had to add one thing.

"Oh and I'd finally prove to you that handles are better than a jumpshot." I added with a smirk. Jaheem rolled his eyes at that.

"Out of everything you said, I think that's the least believable to be real." He responded.

"Yeah, yeah. How about you? You every think about it?" I asked.

"Yeah of course. Mine's pretty similar to yours, except I'd be setting records in basketball, easily smashing the 3 point records, most points in a game record, and points per game record. I'd probably let football go as I'm good at it, but it's not my style, and get a full ride to Texas off of basketball alone. I'd keep good grades, but I'm not going for valedictorian or anything, and I'd focus on my jumpshot clearly. I'd be drafted 1st to the NBA, and take whatever team that was to the finals the next year, winning MVP, Rookie of the Year, and breaking 3pt records in my 1st year. I'd be balling basically, and proving to *you* the superiority of a jumpshot." He said with a smile. I couldn't tell if he believed it or if he was just talking about his dreams as I had. It got quiet for a moment before he spoke again.

"Most of all though, if we could get everything back, I'd probably try to stay with Mom and Dad as long as possible. I know that if this never happened, I wouldn't miss them like I do, but…yeah I'd like to stay with them." He spoke emotionally. I could see what he was talking about too. We would likely never see our parents again, so it made sense to try to get the opposite out of this fantasy life we were talking about. I nodded and agreed.

"Same here." Is all I could say without getting choked up. Another bout of silence fell over us before Jaheem spoke up again.

"You ever think about anything else? Like outside of basketball and Mom and Dad? You was going with Nia right? You think y'all would get married or whatever? Or would you drop her you think?" He asked. It was a weird question. I liked Nia, so I couldn't imagine dropping her. She was smart, beautiful, supportive, and overall a good girl. But at the same time I can't imagine getting married at such a young age.

"I don't know man. I'm too young to think about marriage and all that. I know I would eventually, have a family and all that, but I can't predict if it'd be with Nia. I'd hope it would be, but I can't promise you that." I responded. 'Heem looked playfully annoyed.

"Come on man, it's a fantasy world. Fantasize a bit. I know me, I'd have *all* the honeys until I found the perfect one, likely undercover and not letting them know how rich and famous I am, to start a family with. You telling me you never thought of marrying Nia or never had any type of plans with her?" He asserted.

"Nah. I mean like I said, in a perfect world, yeah it'd be her. I just…never really thought about marriage between us. So I can't really answer. You caught me off guard." I spoke honestly.

"Pssht. You sound like you're just scared to admit you want to marry her. It's alright bruh, it's just us, I'll keep quiet." He teased. I just ignored him and rolled my eyes. I liked that we were now comfortable enough to just sit and talk again, to joke, to tease, to fantasize. It was good to get away from the harsh reality of our situation from time to time. To actually feel comfortable. We got so comfortable that my eyes started getting tired and I yawned in response. Jaheem saw that and urged me to sleep like he did in the first bus terminal.

"Go ahead, I got you. I'll let you know when we're at the border." He said. I just nodded tiredly and closed my eyes as they got heavy with sleep.

"Yo, Jabari! Jabari! We're here!" Is all I heard as my eyes still registered darkness. Slowly I opened them and began blinking rapidly to wake myself up.

"Yo what's happening?" I asked groggily, still recovering from my sleep and getting re-acclimated to the non-sleep world.

"We're here. The border." Spoke my brother in a hushed tone. Ah, the border. We were so close, I could taste it. I shook my head to further awaken myself before speaking.

"Alright so what? Are they making us get off and show our papers?" I asked, hoping for a second that they'd just let it go. With a grim smile, 'Heem let me know different.

"Yeah. So what are we going to do?" He asked, sounding more lost than I'd ever heard him sound before. Jaheem always was ready and always had a plan so it was a bit jarring.

"I...we got to get off the bus and find a way past the border on foot. Like reverse Mexican immigrants." I stated matter-of-factly. He was quiet, with no response. Something else that I wasn't too used to.

"Come on." I said as I beckoned him to walk with me off the bus, much like the other passengers. Only difference is that we weren't coming back.

We walked off the bus silently and stopped to look around. The place was crawling with policemen, at least 20 of them in just the area I could see. I was confused until I remembered that we were wanted men. Not just that, we were wanted murders, cop killers in their minds. It made sense that they took precautions. I saw that the closest cops were only about 10 feet away, questioning the other passengers and accepting their passports and other paper work as proof. I motioned to Jaheem to walk around the bus to the other side so we could get a better view of the border and how to get across.

We snuck around the bus and instantly saw about 10 more cops waiting for us. My breath was caught in my throat for a moment as I formulated a plan. We couldn't go back the way we came, as there were *more* cops on that side, but we also couldn't just deal with 10 cops so easily. Maybe if we walk normally, away from the border they won't bother us? It was worth a shot, and the only thing I had.

"'Heem, let's walk casually away from the border. Hopefully they won't mess with us too much, and we can still scout out the place for an opening and a way over." I relayed to him in a whisper. He nodded before smiling.

"Good, glad you got a plan. I was going to say we taze the driver and steal the bus." He joked with me. I just gave him a look and a smile, before getting serious again. We came from behind the bus slowly and walked away from the border back near some buildings. All seemed to be going well until we heard a voice come from behind us.

"Hey. Weren't you 2 on the bus? Where's your passports?" Said the voice. I glanced over, using my peripheral vision and saw it was the cop from before, the one with the rest of the passengers. I swore internally as I thought of what to do. I looked to Jaheem to see if he had a plan and all he could do was shrug. With a deep breath, I could only say one word which ended up being our new plan.

"Run." Not needing much motivation, Jaheem took off like a bat out of hell towards the buildings, and I went after him. Being the older brother, I was faster and thus had to slow down a bit to keep pace with him. No way were we getting split up in a situation like this. We continued running, making a few sharp turns right, then right, then left, then straight for a while, before turning left again. It seemed like we lost the cop, so we stopped for a moment.

"Damn. Okay, Jaheem, you look to our left and see if there's any cops, I'll look to our right. If it's clear, just say clear. If not, say how many are coming and how close they are." I managed to squeeze out between breaths. Jaheem nodded as he too was catching his breath. "Okay, on 3. 1...2...3!" I said as we both looked around. I saw 3 cops coming from a long ways, over 100 meters. They seemed to be scouting the place out now that we were here. I turned to tell Jaheem, but he spoke first.

"2 cops, 5 feet, run!" He said as he took off running, straight and then taking a right sharp turn. Before I could say much or try to follow him, I saw the 2 cops run by after him, guns drawn. I ran right behind them, but before I could take the right, 2 shots rang out near me, the other cops from the right were firing. The 2 cops turned around once they heard the gunshots and aimed at me, so I had no choice but to dip left and try to lose them, leaving Jaheem alone to fend for himself. A decision I regretted dearly. The cops from the right followed me, but I was too fast, now without my brother and moving full speed. I weaved through the buildings, going left then left, right, straight, right, left again and even exiting the area where the buildings were with no one in sight.

Quietly I snuck back to the border, avoiding the groups of police I saw before, as I ducked down below their sight, and at one point I even had to duck behind the bus again. Before I knew it, I ended up at the border, a tall wall in my way, but nothing I couldn't jump or climb over. The problem was that there was no Jaheem with me. I wanted to message Jaheem, but I didn't want to get him caught at the same time. It'd only been about 10 minutes since we last saw each other, so he might've been near them. I could lose the cops easier being

71

faster, but he might've needed more time. I waited 5 minutes, making sure the coast was still clear and no one was near me, before all-but whispering into the walkie-talkie.

"Jaheem." No response. "Heem." Again, no response. I started to worry and my heart started to fill with dread. Did they get him? Was he in trouble? Did I blow up spot? I wanted to be sure though, so I tried once more. "'Heem, it's Jabari come in." I waited for a few seconds. This time I heard a slight scuffle and what sounded like a gurgle from my walkie-talkie. "'Heem is that you?" I asked desperately, needing to know if my brother was OK.

"...Yeah it's me." Came the response. Thank the Heavens, Jesus, God, Mary, Joseph, Ra, and Odin. My brother was alive.

"Ah shit, you had me worried there for a second. Where are you?" I asked, concerned. Some more garbled sounds came out before he responded.

"...in the back somewhere trying to lay low. I lost 'em but they're still around here somewhere. Where you at?" I smiled at his response. So he was good for now.

"At the border, waiting. You need help? I can run back in and get you?" I relayed to him in earnest.

"Nah, I'm good. Stay there. You made it. Just wait for me and I'll be right out. Don't message me though, they might hear it." He responded. It took everything in me not to rush in there and go against everything he just said. I couldn't just wait for my little brother to get out on his own, it was too dangerous. I was 2 seconds away from sprinting in when he spoke again.

"You coming in will just mess me up. Probably get me caught. They'll follow you to me. Don't sacrifice yourself for me. I'm good." His logic made some sense. Assuming they saw me, I could lead them to him and then we'd both be trapped. I didn't care much about being trapped *with* 'Heem, in fact I preferred it, but I didn't want 'Heem to be trapped in the first place. So I listened and waited. Another mistake I regretted.

I waited at the border for what felt like several life times, and still Jaheem wasn't there with me. 20 minutes passed and I was worried, but couldn't contact him as I could get him caught. 30 minutes I was terrified, but still unable to initiate contact for the same reasons. 45 minutes I was hyperventilating and only kept sane through sheer hope and confidence in my brother. An hour and I was done, I couldn't wait any longer. What made it worse was that the cops, all of them seemed to exit from the area. Either Jaheem got away or they were up to something. That or...no I couldn't think about that. But with the cops all out, now I could communicate.

"Jaheem, you there? It looks like the police are leaving, what happened?" Silence. "Jaheem! You there? 'Heem, do you hear me?" I shouted into my walkie-talkie not caring who heard me at that point. "'Heem! Come in 'Heem! Let me know you're alright!" I screamed into my walkie-talkie, tears threatening to fall at this point. I wait another moment and hear something.

"...'Bari." Was that? It sounded weak but it definitely sounded like my brother.

"...Bari." It came again. Damn it all to hell, was he? No, I had to go find him and save him. Maybe he was just pinned down.

"'Heem is that you? If you can hear me, save your energy, I'm coming to find you." I yelled into the walkie-talkie.

"...D...on't." Was his response. I promptly ignored it as I got to my feet and sprinted back into the area. It only took me about 30 seconds to reach the back of the area, as I ran faster than I'd ever run in my life. I continued my fast pace as I run up and down that sub-section of buildings, looking, searching for my brother. It took me 5 minutes, 4 minutes and 59 seconds too long, to find my brother, on the floor, holding his chest and barely moving.

"Jaheem!" I exclaimed as tears ran down my face. What happened? How could this happen? Why would they do this? He was 14! 14! "What happened?" I whispered more into the air than looking for an answer. He shuffled a bit on the ground before answering in a weak voice.

"I ran...looked around...and didn't see you...had to keep running. They...they shot...missed...kept shooting...kept chasing...hit me...got away." He breathed out. Tears still running down my face, I held his head to my chest, hugging my brother as he bled out.

"Shh...shhh don't talk remember? Save your strength, you're going to live." I spoke quietly, hushing him in the process. "I...I'll have to give myself up, that's it. They'll get you to a hospital and patch you right up." I rambled on. I even shouted.

"We're over here officers! Please, he needs help!" Jaheem shook his head and responded.

"No...you surrender...shoot you too...we both die...Just...take me with you...to Mexico." With each breath he seemed weaker and there was nothing I could do to help him. He was sadly right, if they shot him who was younger, not a threat, and had no weapons on him, then I had no chance even if I did surrender. No weapons...my mind lingered on that for a moment. No weapons. This was my fault. I left Jaheem out here, alone. I left him out here alone after taking his gun from him. If I hadn't...if I hadn't maybe he'd have been able

73

to fire back, maybe he'd be alive and those pigs, those murderers would be dead in his place. I...I couldn't breathe as I thought about it, about how *I* was the cause of my own brother's death. His voice is what snapped me out of it.

"I'm good to go...just need to...to sleep." He said as he began closing his eyes.

"No! 'Heem you can't sleep, you can't. You'll...just stay awake." I pleaded with him, my voice cracking with emotion, my heart breaking and shattering at the scene before me.

"Nah...I'm good. I'm...sorry...love you...'Bari." If my heart was shattered before, this pulverized it into dust. I was done. I couldn't feel anymore. And yet, I could feel nothing but emotions flowing through my body as my eyes flowed with it in liquid form.

"I love you too 'Heem. I love you too."

"Tell...mom...love...her." He said as he gasped once more, closed his eyes and never opened them again. I cried even harder, the tears streamed faster and the emotions amplified a million fold until it all just burst. I moved my hand to his neck, shaking the entire way, feeling for a pulse. There was nothing. Just like there is inside of me. Nothing. I'm burnt out. No emotions, no feelings, just...nothing. Jaheem...he was right the entire time. The pigs just wanted to kill us, and he should've had the right to defend himself, but I took that away. But I didn't kill him, that was those murderous, corrupt, two-faced, soulless pigs. And they would pay dearly.

Filled with an emotionless rage, I reached for both of the guns in my pockets, slowly lowering Jaheem's cold body to the ground. It wasn't truly cold yet, but to me, to one that can no longer feel, to one who was shot in the heart as he was literally, it was the same. In a zombie-like state I rose to my feet, clutching my guns so hard I almost feared I would crush them. Gradually I moved my fingers to the triggers and walked forward, ready to reap vengeance on those who had wrongfully murdered my brother. Due to my frantic screams earlier, there was a group of pigs about 10 meters from me, guns drawn and closing in. Without hesitation I raised both guns and emptied everything they had into the pigs. They died as they deserved to. I took their guns and kept moving.

The sounds of gunshots must have attracted the rest, which was good for me, as it brought more flies to the slaughter. I had no intention of letting any of those pigs live. They didn't deserve it. Another group descended upon me and as soon as I viewed the blue uniforms, I let everything go again, with two guns raised, butchering them all. I wasn't even sure if I was still breathing at that point, as nothing registered to me but to kill those who had wronged. I kept walking, in a straight line out of the housed area and ran into more and more pigs. Each time I merely blasted them before they had time to react, relishing in their deaths as I'm sure they did with my brother's. Each time I took their weapons so I wouldn't run out. By the time I made it out of the area, all were dead. Including myself, at least internally. I paused for a moment, thinking about if I wanted to take Jaheem's body with me. I decided not to, but I did walk back and retrieve his body so it would not be lost in the maze of dead bodies, in the maze of buildings where he died. I picked up his body, not caring if his blood drenched my clothes, and laid him down peacefully, before writing him a eulogy on the sand next to him. 'Here lies Jaheem Wilson, an innocent boy, framed and slaughtered by bloodthirsty pigs. He was righteous until the end. He will be missed.'

I then walked towards the border and calmly climbed my way over the wall. As soon as I did, I just sat there, contemplating, thinking. The old me, Jabari Wilson, would've been appalled at me now. I killed dozens of men without remorse. I wasn't even happy with the deaths, I was closer to sad due to what triggered them. I am a failure, unable to protect my brother. Jaheem, my baby brother was dead because of me! I would never forgive myself. I would never forgive them.

I thought to my mother, my father, and how devastated they would be with this news. How they would rightfully blame me for what has passed. The thoughts cause the rage, the cold and emotionless fury to bubble up in me once more. I knew then what I had become: righteousness, justice, one that is undead with no heart to pump his blood, and no breath in his body.

I will kill again, that I know. I am dead inside besides the feeling of justice and vengeance. If you are an enemy of mine in my way, run. If you are an obstacle in my path, accidental or not, run. If you are an innocent person who has been taught wrong and claim falsely to be my foe, run. If you are in alliance with the unjust, the corrupt law, the murderous pigs, run. If you are a liar, a killer, an agent of death rather than the law you claim to represent. If you are in any way shape or form a pig, a policeman, a cop, an officer. If you even wear a Halloween costume that gives you the skin of a pig for a moment, run. For I will be ready to end you. Never again will this happen. I welcome them to search for me. I will go nowhere and wait for them with open arms. Let them come for me. Never shall I run.

About the Author:

   M.A.N is an aspiring entrepreneur that uses his creative writing and original ideas as an outlet to express his imaginative vision. M.A.N uses his discipline and experiences to provide a world of fun, and at times deep thought for the reader. M.A.N. is also the author of Blade Forged in Darkness: an action-adventure fantasy epic that is unique in its point of view, plot, character progression, and overall experience, He Who Leads: an action-fantasy novel that is a true coming of age story rich in character development, plot, and emotional growth, and 10 Great Tales of M.A.N.: A group of 10 great short stories that are unique in genre and narrative.